I0762256

Prosecutors – LA

THE SUSPECT

SUMMER AUGUSTINE

Pearl Rose Publishing Co.

ISBN No. 978-0-9968686-7-9

Disclaimer

This is a work of fiction. Names, characters, businesses, places, events and incidents are either the products of the author's imagination or used in a fictitious manner. Any resemblance to actual persons, living or dead, or actual businesses, places, events or incidents is purely coincidental.

EDITORIAL REVIEWS

"There is no one in the literary world who can weave a story quite the way bestselling author Summer Augustine can. She makes the law so very intriguing, thrilling, and yes steamy . . ."

– Thrive Global

"Bestselling author Summer Augustine **is a master of the law, and all things thrilling,** . . .

– The American Reporter.

"The law and passion are always on the agenda for bestselling author Summer Augustine**, and she serves up both in the most extraordinary way,**..."

– USA Reformer

TABLE OF CONTENTS

CHAPTER 1

D*oes wine spoil?* Jack Wayne wondered, as his vision blurred and his head ached. Squinting his eyes and willing the pain away, he tried to make sense of the question on his mind: *Does wine spoil?* Then, he was distracted by another question: *Is that her?*

The taste of rancid wine lingering on his tongue, Jack sat lazily in the deep, soft, brown, leather arm chair. He was too far out of earshot to hear what she was saying to the stranger standing just outside of Jack's line of vision, behind the third pillar, in the large luxurious room they had settled in for a nightcap. Jack could see the back of her delicious figure—the one he knew so well, after so many long, passionate nights. But something was different about her—something seemed off. Was it her voice? No. He could hear that same familiar voice, as she spoke to the unfamiliar gentleman on the other side of the room. It was unmistakably her voice, the same one that purred into his ear on so many sensuous nights. But her voice sounded strange to his ears. He just couldn't make out why. Was it the accent? Through further blurring vision, Jack stared at the back of her figure, trying to figure out what was off. Was it her hair? It was longer. How did it grow so long overnight? No, that wasn't it. It was wavier. Wait, no, that wasn't it. The color! It was the color. . . red. Red? Why did her hair look red? Jack wondered if it was the lighting, or his blurring vision. He considered the possibilities as he tried to make sense of his surroundings, while his head throbbed, a terrible pounding throb.

Then he wondered why his vision was blurring. Jack pondered the question through the pain, which made it even more difficult to think.

Jack Wayne calculated silently that he hadn't drank nearly enough to be suffering these side effects. *Does wine spoil?* he wondered again. Staring groggily at the glass of red wine still in his hand, Jack Wayne couldn't get the question out of his mind, despite the persistent counter thought: *How could it? It's already fermented.*

"Jack Darling," he heard her say, as he looked up from his glass. She was facing him now. That face. It was her. Visions of that beautiful face rocking above him, last night, the night before, and the night before that, filled his memory. He smiled.

She walked towards him, slowly, seductively. He watched as her curvy hips swung slightly, as if moving to music only she could hear. Red stiletto heels on her feet, clunking against the marble floor, served as the perfect exclamation point at the end of those long legs. The possibility of spoiled wine forgotten, Jack watched her body move, as she approached him. *It's a wig!* he suddenly realized. *Oh that's hot!* he thought to himself. *She's role playing for me. And I like the sound of this fake new accent on her lips, too,* Jack contrived, as excitement filled his veins.

"Jack Darling," repeated the seductive woman. "You forgot to sign this one."

Jack couldn't remember having signed any documents before, and he couldn't think of what he should be signing now. But the wine, the headache, the blurred vision, the confused thoughts, and the sultry image of this spectacular woman, left him unable to resist her demands.

She forced a pen into his hand and placed the document beneath it. "Sign," she demanded with one word. And he did.

She walked back over to the unknown gentleman. And just before Jack passed out, he thought he heard her say to the stranger, "Don't worry, he won't remember any of this in the morning."

CHAPTER 2

SIX MONTHS EARLIER

Ricky sat in the bank manager's office, looking disheveled, as usual. His grey sweatshirt looked worn out. His jeans were torn, and his brown hair was a mess. It appeared as though he hadn't shaven in days. The smell of marijuana emanated from his clothing. Ricky sat patiently, staring downward, as he listened to Clifford Williams' side of the telephone conversation.

Clifford was on the phone with the trustee who was in control of Ricky's inheritance. Ricky knew that good ole Cliff would fix his problem today. Cliff always did. But it was never any less embarrassing each time he had to come into the bank to ask for the favor. As Ricky shifted uncomfortably in his seat, he heard cliff say:

"Yes, Mr. Tate, I understand. Yes, I know this is the third time this year we've made this request, but the young man has bills to pay. Unless you have time to make each individual disbursement required to pay his ordinary living expenses, it seems that you should continue to fund his personal account, so that he can make those payments himself. Of course, in order to do that, you will have to pay the negative balance, as well."

There was a pause. Cliff looked at Ricky, pursed his lips then frowned, as he listened to the person on the other end of the line. Ricky shifted again, waiting anxiously for an answer.

"$25,000" Ricky heard Clifford say. "Yes, Mr. Tate, that includes all bank charges."

Another pause, as Ricky watched Clifford's facial expressions for some sign of what the trustee might be saying. Clifford grimaced.

"I understand that his regular fixed monthly distribution is $30,000 but if you do not make an additional distribution this month to cover the $25,000 negative balance, you will leave him with insufficient funds to pay his mortgage, food, utilities, etc. He lives in Bel Air, and he pays Bel Air size expenses. The $30,000 distribution is necessary to keep him in the lifestyle, in which his grandfather left him accustomed . . . "

Interrupted by the party on the other line, Clifford paused again. He narrowed his eyes with a tight squint and a more intense grimace, as he quickly jerked his ear away from the receiver. Then, Clifford regained his composure before responding with a very professional tone, "I agree. You make a good point Mr. Tate, yes, yes, his grandfather also would've wanted him to balance his check book; but as I understand the trust documents, it is well within your discretion to make additional distributions, as necessary, to ensure he does not lose his home or suffer any unnecessary discomfort. He assures me, he'll be more careful with his spending next month. When he saw that only $5,000 remained available to him, even though he just received this month's distribution, he was quite shocked... Excuse me, sir? Uh, well, yes, it was just as shocking as the last time,... yes. But he has assured me today that this was a wakeup call. I think you should assist him with an additional distribution this month, and he'll spend within his $30,000 monthly budget going forward."

Another pause. Clifford's face relaxed a little this time. He nodded, and said, "Yes. I can reverse some of the incidental charges resulting from the negative balance. Yes. I'll await your call. How long do you think it will be? Thank you."

Clifford hung up the phone and looked at Ricky, "He said he would call back in five minutes."

"Thanks, Cliff. I really owe you one. You know, things just sort of get away from me sometimes, and I ..."

"Don't worry, Ricky. I'm not the one you need to explain things to. I'm just worried that one day the trustee will tell you to figure out how to pay your $30,000 expenses with just $5,000 in the bank."

"Yeah, that would suck," Ricky said, crossing his feet and relaxing in his chair.

Clifford's computer screen had been opened to Ricky's personal account during the call, in case the trustee had any specific questions. It remained open now, as they waited for the trustee to call back. Clifford looked at the screen and saw the usual spending in Aspen, typical of Ricky this time of year. Making small talk, while they waited, Clifford asked Ricky: "How was your trip to Aspen this year?"

Ricky answered, "Aw, I had to skip that trip this year. Business overseas."

"That's odd," replied Clifford, "There are three weeks' worth of charges at a hotel you frequent this time of year. Did you authorize those charges?"

"I dunno," answered Ricky, in his typically lazy speech, sounding stoned, as usual.

The bank manager furrowed his brow and stared at him inquisitively, prompting further explanation from Ricky.

Ricky replied, "I probably forgot to tell my assistant to cancel the reservation or something."

The phone rang, and Clifford answered. It was the call they were waiting for. Ricky perked up in his chair and watched Clifford intently. He heard him say, "Thank you, Mr. Tate. I appreciate that very much."

Clifford hung up the phone. He smiled at Ricky: "The trustee has agreed to fund your regular $30,000 monthly distribution plus an additional $25,000 to cover the entire negative balance. So don't worry. Your regular $30,000 is entirely available for your personal spending this month."

"That's great! Thank you! Thank you so much, Cliff! I knew you could fix this for me!"

Clifford smiled and looked back at his screen at something else that had caught his attention before the phone rang and disrupted their conversation about Aspen. Still staring at the screen, he pointed at it as he asked Ricky his next question: "Ricky, you say you did not go to Aspen this year, but I see several transactions for large sums of money that could have only been spent by someone physically present in Aspen. Like this one. See?" Clifford rotated his computer screen so Ricky could see what he was pointing at. He looked up to face Ricky, but was surprised to see an empty chair. Ricky had already exited Clifford's office. He looked out the window to see Ricky slipping into his red sports car and speeding away. Clifford shook his head with frustration, and threw up his arms in resignation.

CHAPTER 3

Clifford Williams took his clients' money more seriously than they did. Most of his clients were wealthy young adults whom he still considered to be children, despite the fact that their ages ranged from twenty-something to nearly forty. They were the children and grand-children of the billionaires and multi-millionaires who opened trust accounts for their heirs at the bank Clifford managed in Beverly Hills, California. They banked there because of their long-standing relationship with Clifford, whom they trusted to serve as an unofficial overseer of the accounts. They knew he would keep an eye out for anything suspicious, and would notice if the official trustees weren't handling matters properly.

In addition to trust accounts controlled by official trustees, the children of these wealthy families also had their own personal accounts at the bank. On the first of each month, the trust accounts would automatically deposit a fixed sum into the personal accounts, as a monthly "allowance" so to speak. The heirs and heiresses were able to control their personal accounts themselves so that they could pay for their day to day spending. However, the bulk of their wealth remained safe in the hands of their trustees, who controlled the valve of their steady income stream.

Generations of wealthy families had trusted Clifford to serve in a role, as their friendly, unofficial overseer. It was like having a family member at the bank keeping an eye on their children and their children's appointed trustees. While Clifford had the utmost respect for the older generations, the newest generation of children coming into their own gave Clifford the worst heartache.

This generation was lazy. Too lazy to balance their checkbooks. Too lazy even to handle their own transactions, leaving most of it to their assistants. This generation didn't care how much money remained in their personal accounts at the end of each month, because they knew that the trust account, created by their parents or grandparents, would automatically deposit another large sum into their personal accounts on the first day of the following month. From their perspectives, the well never ran dry; not even when their personal accounts had negative balances at the end of a month.

These over-sheltered heirs wouldn't care about their account balances until their personal accounts reached a negative balance so large, that their guaranteed monthly "allowance" couldn't cover it. That's when they would inevitably come visit Clifford and ask him to work things out with their trustees and cajole them into making an extra distribution into the personal account in order to cover the negative balance.

These frequent visits gave Clifford a complete understanding of his younger clients' habits, lifestyles and schedules. This is what gave Clifford enough knowledge to notice suspicious activity on their personal accounts. For example, spending in Cannes, France, weeks after their annual trips to the Cannes Film Festival would have long-since been over.

Today, Clifford noticed another flurry of suspicious activity relating to multiple accounts of people he knew to be close friends, but who had different trustees and different assistants.

Clifford had grown exasperated with the futility of his prior attempts to alert the account holders of suspicious activity. So, this time, instead of contacting the account holders, Clifford called his friend in the District Attorney's Office.

After two rings, he heard that familiar voice answer, "Jack Wayne." Jack's grandfather had banked at Clifford's branch many years ago, before he lost the family wealth to a long and terrible gambling habit. Before Jack finished law school, the family was nearly destitute. But it didn't bother Jack at all. Jack always had a passion for law enforcement and public service. So naturally, Jack was happy to take his dream job at the District Attorney's Office and stay there for his entire career, never once complaining about the lifestyle he could have had.

When Jack answered the phone, Clifford spoke without introduction: "Hi Jack. I need your help with something."

Jack recognized the voice instantly, and responded without asking who it was, "Anything, Cliff. What is it?"

"I don't know what to do. These kids are so obnoxious. I can't even get them to care about their own money. Well, I guess that's why they don't care, it's not really their money, it's their parents' and grandparents' money."

"Cliff. You're babbling. What is it?"

"Well, I'm noticing suspicious activity in the accounts of a group of my younger clients who bank here. They are all friends with each other; but, they have different trustees and different assistants who might have access to their banking records. So I can't figure out what the connection is or what's happening, but I am certain I'm seeing fraudulent charges on their accounts, all occurring around the same time and in the same places."

"How do you know it's fraud?"

"Well, it's not obvious enough for our automatic fraud detection to pick up. In order to detect it, you would have to know their personal habits. The transactions mimic their behavior—I see the same level of spending at the same locations they frequent, which would easily slip by our automated fraud detection system. But the timing of when the transactions are occurring does not match the clients' schedules. The transactions are occurring either a few weeks after they ended their trips, or for trips they never went on. It looks like the fraudulent charges are premeditated, and it looks like the fraud is being committed by someone they all have in common; but, I don't know of any employee or trustee that any of them have in common."

"Well, have you asked the account holders about the suspicious activity?"

"I have, but they don't care."

"Cliff, if they don't care, how am I supposed to help you?"

"Jack, the total amount of money that's being siphoned by these thieves could buy several luxury homes. It's not pennies we're talking about here."

"I understand. Nobody wants a thief to get away with his crime, but what I'm saying is, if the account holder doesn't care that the money is missing, how will the authorities ever prove it was stolen? It sounds like consent."

"It's not consent. It's stupidity, laziness, ignorance, neglect. I don't care what you call it. But it's not consent."

"Ok, ok. Explain to me how you've drawn your conclusions so that I can analyze the facts to determine whether you might be on to something here."

"Alright. I guess I'll start from the beginning. I grew suspicious after a casual conversation I had with one of my clients while he sat in my office as we waited for his trustee to call me back. I saw what appeared to be a normal flurry of banking activity, which mimicked the client's usual habits during his trips to Aspen. So, I asked the client how his recent trip to Aspen went. And he said he cancelled it due to business overseas, and probably forgot to tell his assistant to cancel reservations. But what struck me as odd was the fact that there were several other charges that could have only been made by someone physically present in Aspen.

When I looked up to ask the client how that could have occurred, I saw that the client had already exited the bank and was climbing into his sports car. I then made all the usual attempts to reach him and alert him to the potential fraud, but the client passed me off to his assistant, saying she'd look into it. The assistant confirmed that all charges were authorized."

Jack interrupted Cliff's narrative, "Cliff, this just sounds like forgetfulness, so far."

Cliff insisted, "No. Jack. You can forget to cancel reservations for a chartered plane, or for a hotel stay, but forgetfulness does not make cash withdrawals at an ATM in a city you're not in."

Jack responded, "Ok. Go on."

Cliff continued: "A few weeks later, I noticed additional suspicious activity in the accounts of several clients, also occurring in Aspen around the same time. Each of the clients referred me to their personal assistants to answer my questions about the charges to their accounts.

"Although each client has a different personal assistant, I could tell that after the assistant answered my call, I was being transferred to someone else. I was transferred to the same female voice, each time; and each time, she approved all charges. None of the assistants told me that I was being transferred. But each time after they answered my call, they would say something like: 'can you hold for a minute, I'm on the other line.' But when the line would pick up again, I heard a different voice answer, pretending to be the personal assistant I called."

Jack interrupted again: "How do you know it was a different person?"

"I'm familiar with the voices of my clients' personal assistants. I'm referred to them frequently when I attempt to reach a client to discuss their accounts, and my clients have had the same personal assistants for years," answered Cliff.

"Ok," said Jack, "That's plausible. But how can you tell it was the same female voice you were transferred to each time?"

"It sounded the same. It was very distinct. Although she tried to hide her accent, she had one. It sounded like it could be British. But I couldn't tell exactly where the accent was from because she intentionally tried to cover it. She would pronounce the "r" in the word "charges" with a strong emphasis, as if she had to make a special effort to pronounce it with an American accent. It sounded forced. It was quite annoying actually, that's how I noticed it was the same voice. I heard the same annoying sound in that awful pronunciation in each call. And in one phone call, she slipped and pronounced the "r" the way a British person might pronounce it, then she caught herself and repeated the word "charges" with that harsh "r" sound, as if she was trying, but failing to sound like an American. It was pretty ridiculous, actually. It was very obvious to me that I was speaking to the same person each time, and that the person's native tongue was not American English.

"Naturally, this all led me to suspect that something was amiss. I hope you agree with my suspicions, but I am unable to confirm with my clients that the charges were not authorized. They simply don't think it's worth their time to address my questions about charges they think are insignificant, despite the fact that each individual charge is large enough to equal an average American's monthly salary."

Jack had listened carefully and thoughtfully to what Clifford described. Normally, a case with such little evidence would not have interested him; but, when Clifford described the same female voice being involved, Jack began to wonder if an organized crime ring was at work. If so, that concern was a matter of public interest, and the mere fact that individual account holders were too wealthy to notice or care, did not mean the authorities shouldn't care. The authorities had to focus on the fact that a possible organized crime ring was threatening the greater community.

"Cliff, here is what I need you to do. It sounds like you know your clients' patterns well. Please create a memo for me which describes their patterns. Then, list for me all the suspicious charges. Give me dates, amounts, places, etc. Then, identify what facts you are aware of that make each transaction suspicious. If you can, list for me the names of all the assistants or other employees you are aware of, who may have access to each client's banking records. I'm sure if my detectives look into it they will find the person in common."

"There is no one in common."

"Cliff, just send me the information, we'll find the link."

"But I can't disclose the client's bank records without a subpoena."

"Well, I can't really subpoena anything. I don't have probable cause."

"But aren't my suspicions reasonable?!"

"Yes. Actually it's funny you use those words. We have what the law would call 'reasonable suspicion.' It's enough for a police officer to stop people and ask them questions. But the higher standard of proof is what the law calls 'probable cause.' I need probable cause before I can convene a grand jury and start issuing subpoenas, very hard to do in a case where I don't even know who the suspect is, and the victims don't even know they are victims. Thus, not enough probable cause."

"Oh, I see," said Cliff, feeling helpless.

"But, you don't have to give me bank records. All you have to do is prepare a memorandum of your personal observations. Don't give me your clients' names or their account numbers. Just write me a story in your own words, like you've done on the phone today, but with all the details, not just the few examples you've already described. Give me the what, when, where, how much and why. But don't give me the clients' names or bank records. All I'm trying to do here is first see the pattern, then link the pattern to a specific suspect. Can you do that for me?"

"Yes. I guess that would be alright."

"Ok then. Send me the information, and I'll be in touch."

CHAPTER 4

Jack Wayne was next in line to become District Attorney of Los Angeles County. He had paid his dues, earned his stripes, and established himself as the most worthy successor to the retiring D.A., who would be announcing his retirement in just six months, while simultaneously endorsing Jack Wayne. The announcement would be made at just the right time to allow Jack to kickoff his election campaign with an endorsement by the outgoing D.A. It was going to be a shoe-in.

Having served in the District Attorney's Office for the past twenty years, Jack Wayne had no other goal in life, than to become District Attorney of the county in which he grew up. He was ready to finally step up to that coveted position. Jack had already been transitioning into a more administrative role during the past five years of his career, not doing much trial work, but instead supervising other prosecutors and leading major crimes teams. He directed teams of prosecutors and police officers in investigating and prosecuting the most heinous crimes that occurred within Los Angeles County.

Occasionally, Jack would handle a trial himself, just to keep his skills fresh. It was his philosophy that he could not lead other prosecutors if he sat out of the game too long to remember what it was like. So today, Jack sat at his desk studying the case he had discussed with Clifford Williams. Jack had the luxury of keeping the most intriguing cases for himself. This was a white-collar crime case, which was complicated enough to warrant referring it to the FBI. But Jack wanted the challenge and the glory. He justified keeping the investigation local, with the excuse that the crime ring appeared to contain its criminal activity within L.A.—targeting the wealthy young residents of Los Angeles County. Also, state law carried a long enough prison sentence that there was no need to turn this into a federal case. But the strongest reason underlying Jack's decision to keep the case, was his need for a new and interesting challenge.

This case intrigued him. It involved a crime ring that selected its victims carefully. Almost like corporate espionage, this crime ring would infiltrate the inner circles of wealthy young heirs and heiresses who made for easy targets. Their carelessness with the vast sums of money they inherited, but which they had never earned, made them easy prey. The easiest prey were the ones who had spent, what should have been their college years, partying, instead of learning how to balance a check book. Their elitist attitudes and exclusive groups deprived them of the opportunity to develop the common sense that naturally develops in others who mingle with the masses, e.g., "ordinary people." The victims' close knit social circles were meant to keep them protected from predators who might capitalize on their lack of awareness, an awareness which less sheltered people learned by simply living life. However, this crime ring knew how to penetrate those tight knit circles; and Jack Wayne planned on penetrating this crime ring.

As he rifled through the scarce evidence the State had gathered so far, Jack's assessment was that there was much work still to be done, before Jack could ever present this case to a grand jury. He closed the file and placed his favorite blue ink pen on top, a habit which indicated that he had finished consuming data and was now ready to process it. Jack leaned back in his chair, with his arms crossed over his strong muscular chest, his square masculine jaw growing more and more tense as his mind fell deep into his thoughts. Jack narrowed his eyes and furrowed his brow, staring straight ahead, without focusing on any object. His thoughts turning inward, mulling over the evidence he had just reviewed, Jack concentrated deeply to prepare a strategy for further developing the evidence.

He thought of who the likely suspects were and began to draw a relationship between them. Thinking of the likely culprits, but not knowing for sure who exactly the real players were, Jack realized, that the prime suspects were people who had penetrated the wealthy young victims' inner circle several years earlier. This group operated slowly but methodically. Their game was to earn the trust of the victims. Trust that would lead the victims to handing them their credit cards or debit cards to book appointments, pay for their services, or purchase their products. The key suspects were also individuals who were close enough to gain access to the target victim's banking information. From Jack's review of the file, it appeared that the suspects had been working together as a team to regularly and repeatedly embezzle funds from a wide range of wealthy victims living in Beverly Hills, Malibu, and Bel Air.

The evidence clearly reflected the behavior of a group of thieves working together. These thieves knew their victims' habits well. They had enough intimate knowledge of their targets, that they could mimic their spending habits so closely, that most of the fraudulent activity would go undetected.

It was likely that the female voice the bank manager heard in each call, was the ring leader. However, so far, there were no clues as to her identity.

Clifford had explained that each of his clients, whom he believed were victims, had had the same personal assistants for years. It was clear to Jack now, that these assistants were working with another unidentified female to siphon money and other luxuries off of their wealthy employers. Jack determined that the assistants were mere pawns. He hoped to use them as witnesses against the mastermind when the time was right. But the investigation was a long ways away from that.

As Jack stared at the closed file with his strong arms still crossed over his muscular chest, he realized that the crime ring was likely using the same tactics that his under-cover police officers used to penetrate gangs and drug dealers' inner circles. He decided to give this crime ring a taste of its own medicine. So, he sat staring at the closed file as if drawing information from it telepathically. He plotted the manner in which he would penetrate the crime ring whose players were only vaguely identifiable. The file Jack stared at contained only bits and pieces of reasonable suspicion. He needed more. A lot more.

Jack thought of his typical under cover officers who were already trained for this sort of thing; but, he couldn't decide which one would work for this role. He needed someone who could pose as a potential suspect who might get recruited by the mastermind or the pawns to join their scheme. The under cover officer would have to become one of the pawns who were already suspects in the case. This included personal assistants, personal trainers, jewelry salesmen and private masseuses—all of whom had been seen in Aspen during the period in question, without their employers/clients. Masseuses had been paid for massages obviously never given. Personal trainers had received travel pay for weeks of one-on-one training they'd never delivered. And all parties enjoyed luxury spending on hotel rooms, dining, and retail shopping in Aspen during a trip from which their employers/clients were absent. Jack presumed that these thieves had arrived in Aspen, courtesy of that charter flight, that Clifford's client, or rather his assistant, 'forgot' to cancel. Jack felt certain that further investigation would reveal that several other charter flights flew the various assistants, and service providers back and forth under the same circumstances.

The pawns' identities were discovered by security footage of the hotels, restaurants and retail shops where the transactions were charged. Clifford recognized three personal assistants who were seen with a group of friends. The friends were linked to the victims with a paper trail identifying what service or product each suspected pawn delivered to the victim. It was too soon to arrest them all for a couple of reasons. First, the unidentified female voice on the phone had been alerted by the fifth phone call made by the inquisitive bank manager. In that call, she stumbled upon her words a little, when the manager asked her how it was possible for the owner of the bank account to be in two places at the same time. In an impromptu cross-examination that Clifford could not resist, he had pointedly stated that he also observed banking transactions in a different state at a different restaurant at the exact same time.

In response, the female voice stuttered a little, but was quick with a plausible excuse. She had said: "Uh, . . . oh, . . .um, yes! That's right. It was a staff appreciation retreat. Mr. Walters wasn't there that trip. He and his friends often plan their own secretary's day, so to speak, and they splurge on a weekend to spoil their staff, who they hope will get along with each other. They always plan it for the same weekend so we can spend quality time together. They say it keeps us loyal to them, and getting along with each other. It's a nightmare when friends' personal assistants and staff don't get along. It's their way of keeping the peace among their entourage."

Clifford could hear the deceit in the woman's voice. He had explained to Jack that the deceit was obvious from her nervous stumbling to her sudden new idea, evidenced by inappropriately timed excitement, as she exclaimed "yes!" at the moment her cover-up excuse had obviously just entered her mind. It was also in the way she became so smooth, as her story rolled on. Clifford explained that he could hear the nauseatingly fake sweetness take over the tone in her voice as she grew more comfortable with her own fabricated story oozing out of her mouth so smoothly once she began giving form to the thought that had sprung into her mind. Clifford explained that all the telltale signs of a seductive woman, who believed she was fooling a man, were clear in her voice as she concluded her spontaneous story.

While Jack was impressed with Clifford's ability to serve as a human lie detector, noting subtle fluctuation in a person's voice, Jack also knew, it was not enough to convince a jury that the speaker was lying.

However, Jack made a note of the provable inconsistency in the woman's statement. Clifford had explained that there were inconsistencies between her statement and the bank records. It was not one weekend, but several weeks of activity. Also, different assistants and personnel were seen on security cameras in Aspen at different times during that period, not altogether at once for a supposed entourage retreat. Jack and Clifford determined that this key suspect, the unknown female voice whom Clifford described, had created the story about a staff retreat in order to provide a preemptive excuse for any questions regarding accounts, about which Clifford had previously inquired.

Though the suspect was very clever in the way she had feigned ignorance of the effect this story had on the other accounts Clifford called about (which were supposedly handled by other people not connect to her), Clifford and Jack knew that she intended to kill several birds with one stone by indirectly persuading Clifford that the other accounts also had a legitimate reason for showing transactions occurring in a state, in which the account holders were not physical present when the transactions were made. However, the weakness in the suspect's clever lie, was in the fact that she had no idea that Clifford had watched surveillance video exposing the extent to which various assistants were involved in the scheme.

Despite Clifford's suspicions, he was unable to provide Jack with a single client who confirmed that the charges in Aspen were fraudulent. This was not due to a lack of effort. His clients simply would not trouble themselves to answer Clifford's questions about the transactions. Whether it was a rebellion against their perceived babysitter, or sheer negligence, the account holders would give vague responses, followed by lapsed memories, followed by the client insisting that the bank manager could rely on whatever their personal assistant had told him.

Clifford had tried his best to alert the various account holders to fraud. In each phone call, he had explained: "but it didn't sound like your assistant on the phone." However, each of his clients had reacted with an unhelpful response. One client laughed,"Nobody sounds the same on the phone." Another client suggested Clifford needed to take some time off. Another client confronted him: "Well, you called the number that's in your records to call, didn't you?" In that conversation, Clifford couldn't even finish his reply to the question, stating: "Well, yes, but. . .," only to have the client interrupt him rudely: "Then it was her! I don't have time for this! Goodbye."

Jack was well aware of Clifford's failed attempts to gain victim participation in this investigation. As Jack continued to ponder the case, he knew that in order to get the wealthy victims to care to press charges, he had to find evidence of larger amounts of stolen funds. He suspected that the pawns were skimming off the top regularly enough, that over time, it actually added up to sums large enough that the victims would care very much. Until he was able to show that, his investigation would be handicapped. He was investigating a crime against victims who would not participate or assist in the investigation. However, Jack was undeterred. The true issue for Jack, was the dangerousness of these perpetrators to become bigger and bolder in their crimes, and to spread their reach to more vulnerable victims. They were already transferring calls to their ringleader, so seamlessly, that further development of their system of theft was bound to occur.

Jack leaned one elbow onto his desk, and rested his chin on his fist, remaining as motionless as the statue, "The Thinker." He remained in that pose, as he thought, . . . and thought, . . . and thought. He kept thinking, . . . *Who should I assign to this under cover job? Who? Who would fit into this crime ring best? Someone enticing. Someone who would draw the suspect to him. Someone the pawns couldn't resist bringing into their circle.*

Then, it dawned on him. He dropped his fist and slapped his desk with both hands as a smile appeared across his face, and he exclaimed aloud: "That's it! I don't need a pawn! I need a victim!"

Jack decided, the best way to lure these criminals to him, was to present them with new prey. Their under cover agent would pose as a new billionaire in town looking for a personal assistant, a jewler, a personal trainer, his own private masseuse—all the usual suspects.

With that epiphany, Jack decided to call it a day. He would consider which under cover police officer to put on the job tomorrow. But tonight, he had to rush home to dress for that fancy dinner his new female of interest had pressured him to attend with her.

CHAPTER 5

Jack slammed the door to his Chrysler 300, a respectably modest car for the public servant that he was. Though he could afford a much more luxurious vehicle, Jack frowned upon the idea of driving a car that some might mistake as too expensive for a public servant's salary. He believed his public image was better served with modesty. After slamming his car door, Jack ran upstairs to his bedroom cursing under his breath along the way. The time was much later than he realized. Always the committed prosecutor, Jack was a workaholic. This was not due to an unhealthy imbalance caused by personal problems; rather, it was the result of his relentless zeal for pursuing justice. Jack was the man in the white hat, and he loved his job. Frequently, while at the office, time would slip away too fast, and he'd forget himself, even on days like this, when he had a beautiful woman waiting for him.

Upon reaching his bedroom, Jack quickly slipped out of his modest business suit, which was typical of what he always wore to the office. He reached into his closet for the silk Armani suit that his ex-girlfriend had gifted him a year earlier. He had only worn it once before. He never saw much need for such an expensive suit. But he quickly dressed in it today because his new girlfriend had specifically requested that he dress particularly well for the occasion. And since he was late, he made sure to dress to impress so that she couldn't also complain about his attire.

Jack wasn't a flashy guy. He didn't need material things to show off. Instead, he allowed his accomplishments and his performance in the courtroom to speak for him, and for themselves. He was a hero. The provider of justice. The man who brought the guilty to their knees. He didn't need fancy things to establish his self-worth. He was more than worthy, of all kinds of praise. He was so committed to serving justice and protecting the community, that he allowed that to be the most important part of life. He worked too hard to be able to maintain a steady or serious enough relationship to lead to marriage.

He was 44 years old and still had never been married. Of course, by L.A. standards, he was still a young man. In L.A., many men remained bachelors until age 50, then married women in their 20s. But those 50-year-old bachelors were usually very wealthy. Though Jack was not a wealthy man, he was established and well-respected. His youthful good-looks also served him well. He never sacrificed a day at the gym, and always maintained a healthy athletic build, which attracted young beautiful women as often as it attracted career women his own age. The career women loved Jack for the combination of eye-candy mixed with a mind they couldn't find in a typical boy toy. Jack was a very hot commodity for career women his age; and he usually enjoyed their company more than the young, hot, mindless creatures who filled the bars of L.A., and were more than eager to date a much older attorney, who they assumed would support them.

In contrast, for established career women, who also lacked the time to develop a healthy relationship with their equals, Jack filled the fantasy of dating a young hot fireman, while also providing the prestige of dating an attorney. He also fulfilled them with the satisfaction of enjoying the company of an intelligent man. It was never difficult for Jack to find female companionship on any given evening.

Tonight, Jack had a date with a 40-year-old workaholic who, much like himself, had always worked too hard at her career goals to give marriage a chance. The difference between him and her, was that she worked for money, and he worked for glory. Jack was happy to earn a public servant's salary, as long as he was serving truth and justice, and winning most of his cases. But Jillian worked at a large private law firm, where she had made partner long ago, and was in a constant race to amass as much wealth as possible, forever competing with the men in her field. Jack knew it was the snobbery, which came with that territory, driving Jillian's request that he dress "particularly well," for the event he would accompany her to tonight. Having dated her kind before, Jack understood that the one and only Armani suit that hung in his closet, would be sufficient to satisfy her request. It was still there from his prior relationship, which ended with Jack hollering at her in frustration, "I'm not your god-damned 'Ken Doll!'" He used to find the behavior of women like Jillian, offensive and emasculating. But he liked Jillian's company, and chose to overlook this same annoying trait in her, so that he could enjoy the other perks of the relationship. Unlike his ex, Jillian was a wildcat in the bedroom.

This made up for all the snobbery, pretentiousness and materialistic attitude she would sometimes portray when she needed him on her arm to impress colleagues of her world. So tonight, he was willing to play the role of intelligent eye-candy, so that Jillian could one-up the men she competed with, who would have mere eye-candy on their arms—the kind that was obviously there for the gold-digging, instead of true romance. These were the men Jillian would emasculate by comparing Jack's accomplishments as an attorney to theirs, for they may have made more money, but none of them could imagine performing in the courtroom as magnificently and gloriously as Jack. Next to Jack, they didn't even feel like real lawyers, they just felt like expensive paper-pushers. It didn't bother Jack, how Jillian would flaunt him competitively, as if he were her newest Ferarri, because afterwards, Jillian would always show her appreciation in ways that left a man willing to put up with anything.

Jack dressed quickly, then slipped on the expensive pair of shoes that his ex-girlfriend had selected for the suit. They were uncomfortable, but he wore them anyway, because he wasn't sure which of his other shoes were fancy enough to pair with the expensive suit. It was safer to simply trust his ex-girlfriend's judgment, assuming that the reason she gifted them along with the suit was because they matched. Jack ran down the stairs in a hurry, as he texted Jillian: "On my way." The pressure he felt on his feet from the tightness of the shoes that had not yet been worn-in, reminded him to be on his best behavior at the snob-party so that Jillian would thank him in the bedroom later—because that was the only thing that made these shoes worth the discomfort.

The uncomfortable shoes were still irritating him as he peeled out of his drive way. "You better put-out, Jillian," he absent-mindedly murmured, while speeding away, as he wondered how long they'd have to stay at the party before going back to her place.

When Jack got to Jillian's place, he pulled into the drive and rang the doorbell. A limo was parked in her drive. The driver exited the vehicle and opened the rear passenger door. Lillian's head popped out and he could hear the annoyance in her voice as she called out to him, "Are you coming?" He hopped off her entry way and rushed down the steps to where the limo was parked. As he approached, Lillian's previously annoyed face, melted into a warm smile. Her eyes lit up as they traced the expensive suit right down to his shoes. "My, my, my, Mr. Wayne. You are dressed particularly well, tonight," she purred, with a deep, sultry voice of approval.

Jack smiled and leaned in for a kiss. She kissed him back, then scooted over to make room for him to join her in the limo. Jack decided this wasn't the right time to ask how long they had to stay at the party. So, he remained silent and turned his broad smile on her. Dazzled by his smile, she completely forgot that he'd kept her waiting so long that she almost had to leave for the party without him.

The limo wound up the windy hill, and kept climbing until it reached the top of a cliff in Malibu. The home was surrounded by lush gardens, vibrant, bright colored flowers and ample vegetation. Tall palm trees lined the ominous iron gate, which surrounded the gardens. At the gate's entrance, was a security booth where the limo stopped to announce its passengers: "Jillian Smart, plus 1," said the driver. The security guard in the booth nodded and buzzed open the gate.

Beyond the gate, stretched more windy road to climb. It was a narrow path, surrounded by trees and shrubs, with small gaps in between, giving the passengers a glimpse of the ocean, which in the darkness, could not be seen, but for, the sparse street lights illuminating the white tips of crashing waves below the high hill. It was a romantic drive up the hill. Jack silently thought to himself, that the car ride was probably going to be more pleasant than the party; but he reminded himself to be a good sport so that he would get his payoff with Jillian when they finally got back to her place. She was already getting frisky in the limo. He silently hoped that nothing at the party would change her mood.

Exiting the vehicle, Jack did not wait for the driver to open their door. He was unaccustomed to such treatment, and felt silly, waiting in the back until someone opened the door for him. Jillian gently complained, "Relax Jack. It doesn't look right to open your own door."

Mildly annoyed, Jack said nothing. He exited the vehicle, turned towards Jillian, forced a smile onto his face, and bowed ceremoniously. "My dear, I am at your service," he joked, as he extended his hand to help Jillian out of the car. This made Jillian giggle, and the tension was eased. As she stood, he kept her hand in his, then brought it to his lips with a gentle kiss. This made Jillian smile more broadly.

"Allow me to be the chivalrous one, Jillian."

"Oh, of course, Jack. I'm sorry. Forgive me," she said gently.

Jack smiled. He could win over a woman as easily as he could win over a jury, always keeping his emotions in check, and never losing his composure.

Jack walked Jillian, arm in arm, up a slate stone staircase, lined with short marble pedestals, connected by dipping iron railings, which curved elegantly between each pedestal. The top of each pedestal was adorned by 12 inch statues of cupid, striking a different pose in each statue. In one statue, cupid pulled back his bow, loaded with an arrow, ready to strike his target. In another, he lounged lazily against a tree, while his bow lie on the ground nearby. In yet another, cupid smiled mischievously as he reached with his right hand for the arrows stored behind his back, while holding his bow in his left hand, stretched out in front of him.

Jack's quick mind—sharpened by years of making instant judgments about surprise defense witnesses in the courtroom—immediately calculated that this homeowner had a strong disposition for romance. Jack smiled, and was now curious to meet the owner. *A man or a woman?* he wondered, silently. Attempting to make the party more interesting, he wagered with himself. *A man,* he bet. Then asked himself, *Why?* Jack sensed a masculine personality, from the domineering and overpowering presence of the home, which sat atop the hill as if demanding that it were king; but the romantic scene surrounding the home, was something he attributed to a more feminine trait. Jack silently assessed the personality of the homeowner, *Strong, powerful, domineering, yet romantic.* He inventoried the characteristics. *A man,* he confirmed, then continued his silent assessment even further, *likely a womanizer who strategically decorated his home with strong romantic allure in order to make it that much easier to get his prey across the finish line, which of course, ended at the threshold of his bedroom door.* As Jack concluded his assessment, he and Jillian reached the grandiose double doors, and rang the doorbell.

A butler answered and ushered them towards the ballroom, where the buzz of mingling voices hummed happily down the long hallway through which they were escorted.

"Jillian! Darling! How are you?" a large framed man greeted them. His muscular physique showed clearly through his tight, pink, button down shirt.

Damn! thought Jack. *How did I miss that one? A gay man, of course!*

The man in the pink shirt approached Jillian, still booming a lavish and exuberant greeting, complete with air kisses for each cheek, "I thought you'd never get here! Thank you for blessing my humble abode with your fabulous presence," he teased her adoringly. Linking her arm into his, he pulled her deeper into the party, almost forgetting that Jack was even there. Jillian turned her head to look back over her shoulder, reaching towards Jack with her free hand. "Jack!" she called out to him.

"Oh! Sorry, Darling!" exclaimed the homeowner, "Did you bring someone?"

They stopped abruptly, and swung around so that they were facing Jack again. Jack had remained standing in the same spot they had left him. He smiled a warm, friendly smile, despite his feelings of annoyance.

"Boy, he's a dish, isn't he?" whispered Jillian's companion in her ear, "Where'd you find this one?"

Jillian elbowed him gently to quiet him down, "The District Attorney's Office. Behave yourself!" she whispered back. Her companion's mouth dropped open in surprise as his eyes traced Jack from head to toe. He had expected her to say he was an aging model, who still found work in commercials filling more mature roles, but he had not expected her to say he was a prosecuting attorney. Jillian smiled triumphantly at her companion. "On his way to becoming THE D.A.," she added.

The pair walked towards Jack, and Jillian's companion extended his arm, "Pete Farwel. Pleased to meet you. Welcome to my home."

Jack shook Pete's hand, "Thank you. Nice to meet you, too."

"Please, come in," said Pete. "Let me introduce you to our newest partners at the firm. This party is for them. Jillian was supposed to give the toast. She gives the best welcome to partnership speeches. But she was so late this time, I had to give them a quick congratulations and get it over with. Now it's time to party!" He raised his glass to emphasize his point.

As the threesome immersed themselves into the crowd of mingling people, Jillian made her introductions to all the appropriate people, which meant, the highest earning partners in her firm. First, Jack was introduced to a man in his 60s who had a 20-year-old model on his arm. Then, a man in his 50s who boasted that his date had won Miss Universe a few years earlier; then another man who was eager to tell them about the nutrition plan his personal trainer kept him on, which changed his life. The personal trainer was also his date to the party. She was a small framed, blonde haired, muscular woman with an Eastern European accent. She came complete with fake eye lashes, fake lips, and fake breasts. Jack wondered what exercise routine she prescribed for her male clients, but was courteous enough not to ask. The woman's name sounded familiar. Too familiar. He thought he'd heard it in the courtroom before. As the man chattered on happily about his nutrition plan, the personal trainer stroked Jack's arm and purred into his ear: "I can put you on plan, too," she said, more seductively than Jack thought a personal trainer ought to be when promoting her business. Then he remembered. *A prostitute.* She had been accused of prostitution and grand larceny by a man's ex-wife who claimed she had swindled him out of a large sum of money, which was meant to be transferred to his ex-wife, within weeks of its disappearance. There had been insufficient evidence to charge the crime, but Jack remembered the suspect's name.

As he debated whether, when or if, it would be appropriate to alert the jolly man of this potential threat, the personal trainer began to lay it on even thicker, as she sought Jack's attention. She began behaving like a peacock fluffing its feathers. She took a step back to give Jack a better view of her body, then stood up straighter, forcing her shoulders back which lifted her fake breasts up. Then she bent one leg, and tilted her chin to the side, and held that position, for an unnatural length of time, as if posing for a picture that nobody was taking.

When she spoke to Jack again, she started with flattery. Inching closer, she placed her hand on his arm again. "Oh. Strong arms. You do not need a trainer, just good company," she winked.

Jack watched her, intently.

"I could give you good company, while you train," she batted her unnaturally long eyelashes. She continued stroking his arm as she spoke. Then, her eyes widened as she realized how expensive his suit was. She couldn't hold back the greedy thoughts calculating in her mind, "Very nice, suit. It is expensive, no?"

And with that one question, the wheels in Jack's mind began to turn. *Bait! That is exactly what I need to draw in members of the crime ring!* he thought to himself. Suddenly, he looked at the personal trainer with renewed interest. *Could she be part of the same crime ring?* Jack wondered. Just before he could ask her another question, her date whisked her away. And Jack suddenly became more interested in the party. He looked all around him with realization. Gold diggers, con artists, embezzlers, they all lurk around the wealthy. And the party was filled with wealthy people. Jack gazed around the room, viewing it now in a different light. He now made it his mission to test how a wealthy person might fall prey to this type. So, he began to walk the walk, and talk the talk.

Jack smiled brightly as Jillian introduced him to another colleague. Normally, it annoyed him when she paraded him around like the best prized horse in the room—the one that could actually do tricks. But tonight, he relished the attention. Tonight, he would strike up conversations with the corresponding eye candy that Jillian's peers brought to the party. He fell back on his experiences from his old life, before his grandfather lost the family fortune. When he heard Jillian's competitors brag about their yachts, Jack would talk about his family's yacht (leaving out the part about its unfortunate liquidation). When he heard them discuss their world travel, he would chime in about the places his grandfather used to take him. It worked. Like a magnet, he drew every opportunist in the room.

And, that is when Jack knew. . . The perfect undercover agent, which he was looking for to investigate the crime ring, was himself.

CHAPTER 6

Gil Ramirez was a talented young detective who worked more undercover jobs than most men his age. He was 30 but could pass for 21. He had such a great talent at playing his undercover part, that he could infiltrate gangs, organized crime, and the network of drug dealers who'd been on his agency's most wanted list for decades. His arrest rate far exceeded any other officer in his department. And the conviction rate that followed these arrests was 100%. He was so talented at playing whatever role his undercover job required, that many of his comrades teased him at being in the wrong business. They nicknamed him "Hollywood" because they thought that's where he should be—on the silver screen. Gil hated the nickname. He thought it made him sound like a pretty boy—which was another trait he'd been teased about most of his life.

Jealous friends who had watched, more often than they could stand, how Gil could make any girl melt with just one smile, would make themselves feel better by teasing Gil about his natural good looks. Gil had a solid, but small frame. He was fit, muscular and fast. He wasn't tall and he wasn't short. His ethnic background gave him a warm skin tone that looked like he had the perfect tan all year round - which served to emphasize his perfect, stark white teeth and dazzling smile. Although he wasn't a large man, his facial features were strikingly masculine. He had a narrow but square jaw, full lips on a wide mouth, two perfect dimples on his cheeks, and dark brown eyes that could capture any woman who dared look into them. His face was a blessing and a curse. For the line of work he chose, he had to roughen up his look in order to fit in with the baddest and most dangerous criminals. He did this with a scowl and a glare that could put to shame any "resting bitch face." Except, this wasn't "resting bitch face." This was resting "I want to kill you face." It convinced all criminals who accepted him into their fold, that he was a hardened enough criminal, that he could be trusted.

But today, Gil was not undercover. His beautiful features were shining today as bright as the Southern California sun. Today, he let a soft expression own his beautiful face. It came easy for him. He needed to charm the woman in charge of the cars at the impound lot.

"I think the government is going to auction these," the woman insisted, trying to stand her ground.

"No. They let us use them when we go under cover," Gil argued gently while flashing a beautiful smile.

"I don't know... My boss said the most expensive ones have to be sold, so we can keep more funds for the police department. He said you guys don't need a $2-3 million car to do your undercover work. You can use the $200,000 car and still impress the car thieves."

"We're not trying to catch a car thief."

"Who are you trying to catch?"

"I don't know," Gil said absent-mindedly, eyeing the bright blue Bugatti on the lot.

"How could you not know who you're trying to catch?"

"It's a long story," Gil trailed off as he hurried over to the Bugatti, "Give me the keys to this one."

"I can't," the woman insisted.

"Come on, sweetie," Gil turned up the charm, "For this case, we need the Bugatti."

The woman hesitated.

Gil walked towards her with his warm smile. He stood as close to her as was possible without touching. He looked down into her face, stared directly into her eyes, then brought his lips close to her ear. When she caught her breath, he whispered seductively, "It's important police work. A really big fish we're after. You have to help me out."

Five minutes later, Gil was peeling out of the impound lot with a wide grin spread across his face. He sped down the street as if he himself were trying to out-run the police. He took the long way to the Bel Air mansion that Jack Wayne had already rented with money seized from drug deals. This car was too nice to hand over so quickly.

As Gil pulled into the drive, he put the bright blue Bugatti in park, then revved the engine several times. When he saw Jack come out onto the balcony above him, he backed out the drive, shifted gears, then peeled out as he sped down the road.

"Get back here!" Jack shouted, throwing the hand towel he'd been drying his hands with in the direction of the speeding car.

Gil laughed at Jack's reflection in the rear view mirror, and sped around the gated community until he came back around to the mansion that would be Jack's home for the next several months, or for however long it would take to catch the unknown crime boss.

By the time Gil reached the mansion, Jack was standing in the drive with his arms crossed like an angry father waiting for a delinquent teenage son who'd broken curfew.

Wearing his dark sunglasses, ripped blue jeans and a perfectly snug and fashionable t-shirt, which showed off his fit frame, Gil stepped out of the car with a playful smile. He gestured toward the vehicle and said, "You told me to get the best one on the lot!"

Jack walked towards him nodding. He shook Gil's hand and gave him a pat on the back. "Well done. Well done."

"So what part do I get to play?" asked Gil with the excitement of a teenager coming off the thrill of a joy ride.

"I don't know, maybe you could be my butler."

Gil's charming smile fell to a frown, "What!"

"I'm kidding, relax. I haven't decided how to use you yet, or if I'm going to need you at all. I just came up with this plan last night."

"Let me be your spoiled rich son. I saw a tricked out Lamborghini. Let me go back and get it."

"No. I have to be a lonely billionaire lost in L.A., looking for a west coast entourage."

"Those guys don't travel alone! Come on, you have to let me play a part in this. Let me go get that Lamborghini before they sell it."

Jack rubbed his chin and stared at the extraordinarily expensive car parked in his new drive way. It was a long thoughtful stare, as he tried to glean inspiration from the shiny blue Bugatti glistening in the sun. The wheels in Jack's mind turned, as his eyes took in every inch of the car. Then, he began to think out loud, "I guess you can be my overpriced personal business manager. I need someone who might be willing to steal from me. Then, we'll have predator and prey on this job. That way, you might be able to infiltrate the pawns, after I lure them in, using myself as the bait. If you can gain their trust, they might introduce you to their boss."

"Yes! I'll go get the car, now!"

"Wait. I don't think you should be driving a Lamborghini. You need to be underpaid enough to look willing to steal. Also, I think business manager might be a little too far above the heads of the pawns we've identified. We need a better fit. Someone they view as their peer."

"Fine. I'm a glorified assistant. And the Lamborghini is yours. You just let me drive it because you're such a rich snob, you can't even let your staff be seen in anything less."

Jack threw his head back with a hearty laugh, "You really want to drive a sports car for a few months, don't you?"

Gil flashed his winning smile, and turned both of his palms up with a shrug, "Of course I do!"

"Fine," said Jack with a resigned laugh, "Go get it."

CHAPTER 7

Her hair was long, thick and dark. It fell down her tall back just barely brushing the top of a firm, perky backside that captivated most. She was almost six feet tall, with long shapely legs. Her breasts were large, round and firm. Her waist was small. Her hips were perfectly curved with just enough width to compliment her large breasts, while still maintaining a slender figure.

It didn't matter what she wore, or how she talked. What mattered most was the swing of her hips. That subtle swing would draw a man's eyes to that part of her body that triggers his instincts to automatically calculate the ratio between her waist and her hips, which instantaneously triggers his primal instinct to breed her. She usually called herself Venus. Today, she went by "Katherine."

She sat across his desk with tall perfect posture, in a dress wrapped so tightly around her curves, that the gentleman behind the desk could not help but wonder what it would feel like to trace his hands along the same lines. The material of the dress was red, and looked soft to the touch. He couldn't tell if it was satin or silk or a very fine velvet. It just looked very soft and smooth. As smooth as her milky white skin. She leaned in and his eyes widened without his realization. But she saw it, and she heard him catch his breath. She paused for a few seconds while his eyes rested on her cleavage, then she leaned ever closer, reaching for his printer.

She lifted the one page that had just come off as she exclaimed with delicate sweetness, "Oh! This is it! Just give me one moment to check it."

When she placed the page in her lap below his desk, she looked into his eyes and smiled. He stared into her deep blues, the ones she claimed to have inherited from Queen Victoria, down a long line of blue eyed beauties whom the Royal family could never recognize, given the circumstances of the birth of her ancestress.

She waited for him to say, "Queen Victoria, huh?" before she made the swap. Holding his gaze, she exchanged the page from his printer with the one she brought with her. Then, she cast her eyes away shyly as she nodded. Feeling his eyes fixed to her face, she brought forward the page in her hand and gleefully stated, "It's done! The wire is confirmed!" as she handed him the page she brought with her. As he took it from her hand and inspected it, she quietly slipped the page from his printer into her purse—the one that said the wire transfer had been initiated, but instantly cancelled, and therefore no transfer made.

"Congratulations, Katherine!" the car salesman beamed, as he stood to walk around his desk. She met him at his chair before he could get far. Her approach was more than welcome, as he handed her the keys to a brand new Bugatti. "The car is yours," he said, "and what a magnificent color you've chosen, it is as blue as your eyes." He leaned in for a hug, and she indulged him, pressing her soft breasts into his chest as she pressed her cheek against his like a cat purring against its owner. As she did this, she tapped one key on his keyboard, deleting the email he had just printed. Then, as suddenly as she had embraced him, she released him.

"I must go!" she cheerfully declared and slipped away.

He watched until she was out of sight, still mesmerized by her body, her story, and her eyes.

CHAPTER 8

She knew she should've driven straight to the warehouse a few miles from the dealership, where a shipping container awaited. It was to take her only 15 minutes to drive the car right into the container, which would then be placed on a semi-truck headed to Long Beach, where it would be loaded onto a ship to China, where the VIN number and license plate would be changed, before it was flown to Dubai, and sold to one of her many royal customers from the Middle East.

In Dubai, she was not the descendant of a bastard child of one of Queen Victoria's sons. In Dubai, she was a shipping heiress. Being a shipping heiress explained how she was able to import every luxury good that any of her royal clients desired. They knew her only as, "Venus." She would never give her last name, explaining that her father always kept her identity a secret, because neither his first wife, nor his second wife would ever forgive him, had they ever discovered her existence (as she was born to neither of them, but to a mistress). She would tell them, her small shipping company was his gift to her before he died, which he disguised as a sale so that his legitimate heirs would not question it. She could not reveal her identity without jeopardizing her business. Her clients asked no other questions. They made their assumptions about her identity, given that she was named after a Greek Goddess, and her father was a shipping Tycoon. She was too beautiful and too wealthy for any of her clients to dare insult her with any further questions.

The armed guards who accompanied her wherever she traveled also served as a deterrent to her clients prying any further. It was a Muslim country, and they assumed she used armed guards, instead of the hijab, to protect her beauty. They respected that about her, and therefore were not offended or even curious about the presence of her armed guards.

The royalty from various countries that spent their time in Dubai were accustomed to exploiting others, and had no concern for the source of the luxury items Venus sold them. They believed themselves to be above any laws, anywhere they traveled, so the question of any possible criminal connection never even crossed their minds. They didn't really care how an item got to them, just as long as it got to them. This dynamic made them easy clients for her to serve. This Bugatti she now daringly drove out on the open road, longer than she should have, after tricking the salesmen, would fetch her about $3 million. She didn't want to drive it back to the warehouse just yet. She wanted to extend the thrill of her most recent take. It had been far too long since she pulled a job herself. She had spent too long directing others, and allowing her minions to risk their own liberty pulling a stunt like this. But life had become too easy, and she was bored. Also, she wanted to prove to herself that she still had it. It had been at least a decade since she'd performed such a low level task. But it was fun! And daring! And it made her feel alive! But it also meant she had to leave L.A., and couldn't come back for a long, long while.

The thought of leaving L.A., was interrupted by a magnificent spark from up above. As Venus pulled into her gated community in Bel Air, she saw him standing on his balcony, his muscles glistening in the sun. Her mouth dropped open and her eyes became wide. For the first time ever, she understood how men felt when they looked at her. The Bugatti she drove came to a screeching hault, just before nearly colliding with a white Mercedes. The driver swerved, cursed at her out his window, then sped by. She put her car in park, oblivious to the angry man or how close she had just come to possibly losing $3 million, and she stared up at Jack Wayne.

As she watched him, pacing back and forth, shirtless in the sun, she realized that it was more than just the sunlight beaming onto his strong muscular body. There was something else that made that man shine. What was it?

What was that flash that caught her eye? Was it an expensive watch? He wasn't wearing one. Other jewelry? None. A glass reflecting light? He wasn't holding one. Quite possibly, . . . it was just his aura. But Venus didn't believe in that stuff. She kept her gaze upon him for as long as she could. She watched every simple move he made. She could see a treadmill through the window behind him, and some weights stacked on a rack. He had a small white towel thrown over his left shoulder and a cell phone in his right hand. *Who was this man*? she wondered. She pressed a button and her window came down. She put her left ear to the wind hoping it would carry the sound of his words, as he spoke into his cellphone. She heard his voice, but could not make out his words. It was a deep, soothing, masculine voice, the kind that made her instantly feel at ease, relaxed, calm. She wanted to hear more of that voice. But how, she wondered. Her plan was to leave LA, and not come back until after the statute of limitations expired on auto theft. By then, no police resources would even be used to try to find her, even if the car dealership was successful in convincing the police that this incident was more than just a civil dispute.

Venus pondered her options as she watched this magnificent man pace back and forth on his balcony, speaking into his cellphone with such enthusiasm and force that she could see he was a passionate man, by nature. She hadn't seen anyone exude such natural passion in many years. She instantly calculated that this man was passionate about everything in life, his work, his hobbies, his family, the people he loved, and any woman he would love. He was forceful in his speech, but not angry or excited. She could tell he was giving orders. Calculating further, as was her custom upon first sight of anyone, Venus could tell that this was a man in charge of others. Who was he? She had to know. The only thing that rivaled Venus' interest in money, was passion mixed with power.

In that moment, Venus did something completely out of character. She decided he was worth it. So, she made her own phone call and gave her own orders. It was to her contact at the bank: "Type an email. Just type it, don't send it. Address it to the salesman at the dealership. Type only two words: 'Wire Confirmed.' Then print it and put it in the file."

"But that won't do any good, because . . . "

"Shut up," she said firmly, "and just follow orders. It's enough to turn this into something the police would call, 'a civil matter.'

CHAPTER 9

The invitations each guest received were nothing short of class itself. In elegant white, with raised silver font, typed in calligraphy, the invitations addressed each home owner in the neighborhood by name. On the inside, the invite stated:

You are cordially invited to an evening of Champagne and Caviar at the home of your neighbor, so that we may all welcome and befriend our newest neighbor.

Attire: Black Tie

The manner in which each invitation was delivered was even more impressive. A very tall man, dressed in the black uniform of an old fashioned butler, complete with white gloves, delivered each invitation on a gleaming silver tray. He even bent slightly, with an ever so subtle bow, when the home owner was called to the door by their own staff to receive the special delivery. Also on the tray was a custom made party favor in the form of a miniature champagne bottle with a picture of the home at which the party would be held. The picture popped with elegance on a stark white label, and was drawn with the same raised silver ink as used in the invitations. To top things off, macarons accompanied the miniature champagne bottle, one macaron for each guest residing in the household to which the elegant invitation was addressed.

The invitation that was delivered to Jack Wayne was different from all the other invitations. Jack's invitation was addressed as follows:

To The Guest of Honor: Jack Smith

Welcome to the neighborhood.

You are cordially invited to an evening of Champagne and Caviar at your neighbor's house to meet and mingle and be welcomed by the neighborhood.

The guest of honor also received a regular sized bottle of champagne, with a specialized label. The front was the same as the miniature bottles, but the back of the label had another drawing. It was the silhouette of Venus, in the dress she planned to wear at her party, in a pose which emphasized the pure raw femininity of her deadly curves.

The butler, as he was instructed to do, gave a more pronounced bow when delivering Jack's invitation—one that was unmistakably a bow. It was the kind Queen Victoria would've received from her own butler delivering her a message on a tray.

"Well, what do we have here," Jack said aloud as he reached for the champagne bottle, which was strategically positioned on the tray in such a manner that Jack would see the back of the label first. Jack stared at the woman on the label, and his mind wandered to things only natural for a man's mind to wander, upon the sight of such a beauty, teasingly offering only her silhouette. More than just the curves of this beauty on the champagne bottle, was the long thick hair that looked almost as if it were moving. Jack could picture it move with the turn of the woman's head, to reveal the rest of her body, now covered by her long hair. It was the gentle feminine movement of a woman lifting her chin in laughter that Jack imagined as he stared at the bottle.

Jack's thoughts were interrupted by the butler clearing his throat before he said, "The invitation, sir."

Jack looked up at the butler who nodded towards the tray. Then Jack looked down and saw it. "Oh, yes. Yes, of course. Thank you. I appreciate this very much," Jack thanked the butler and lifted the invitation and one single macaron off the tray. The butler bowed again, "Good day, sir," he bid Jack, then swiftly turned to walk away.

Tickled, Jack watched the butler walk towards the house two doors down the street.

Upon closing his own front door, Jack looked closer at the invitation. Before even noticing that he was named as the guest of honor, he stared at the name: "Jack Smith." For the first time, he wondered if Gil was right. Gil had insisted that, while undercover, Jack needed a different first and last name. Jack refused. He argued that if he failed to answer to a fake first name, it would blow his cover. Gil finally yielded, on the ground that "Jack" was a common enough first name, that it was ok to fold to Jack's authoritative stubbornness on this one issue. Knowing that Jack was too accustomed to giving orders, Gil gave up trying to convince him to take the advice of a seasoned undercover cop.

***

One week after receiving the extravagant invitation, Jack had his assistant, Gilbert Johnson, drive him to the party in style. When Gil's undercover name had been selected, Jack had also insisted that Gil use his real first name, so that he too would not fail to respond when called. When Gil reminded him that he'd never done that on any of the many undercover jobs he'd pulled in the past, Jack conceded that the real reason was so that Jack wouldn't accidentally call him by his real first name, instead of a different cover name.

Jack had instructed Gil to tell people his name was Gilbert Johnson, and that they could call him Gil for short. Gil protested the selection of the surname. "Johnson! Johnson! Do I look like a Johnson to you? Look at this face!" he had said while pointing at his own beautiful face, "does this complexion say 'Johnson' to you!" Jack had roared with laughter in response, "I'm sorry, Gil. You gotta put the hot latin lover image away. You're latino when you work other kinds of jobs. To be effective for this sting, I have to yank you out of your ordinary role and make you an entirely different person. I'm sorry. For this one, you just have to be a white guy with a really great tan."

"Well, I'm not dying my hair blonde!" Gil had protested even further.

"No, no, ha, ha, ha" Jack had laughed, "I won't make you do that. A little lighter brown though, just so that anyone who knew you from the last job can't recognize you."

Gil argued, in amusement, "Bel Air is a little far from East L.A., Jack."

"Hey, just do as your told," Jack had commanded gently, "Drastically changing your look comes with the territory."

"What about you?" Gil had teased, "Can we make you a redhead?"

"Hell no!" Jack said, "I don't have to change my look. I've never been undercover and I don't do press. Not yet anyway. Not until we announce my run for D.A."

By the evening of Venus' party, Jack and Gil were firmly and comfortably settled in their new roles. Gil drove Jack the short distance to the large mansion two houses down the street from the one they were occupying.

Gil parked the Lamborghini that Jack had allowed him to drive, stepped out, walked around the car and opened Jack's door.

"Stop it!" Jack commanded him. "Your my assistant, not my gay lover!"

Gil laughed out loud, "I thought this is what driver's were supposed to do."

"No. damn you. Only a limo driver. Not an assistant driving his boss' Lamborghini."

Still laughing, Gil apologized, "Sorry man. Not the type of under cover job I normally do."

"Get out of here," Jack demanded, as he walked towards Venus' front door.

Still laughing, Gil jumped back in the Lamborghini and sped down the road, but not in the direction of Jack's new house. Since Jack was working alone tonight, Gil was going to enjoy that baby for a night out on the town. He figured Malibu would be a good place to pull up to a bar in a Lamborghini. So he sped away, ready to enjoy the night.

***

When Jack entered the room, the neighbors were already abuzz with the liveliness of a successful party. Sheer elegance surrounded him. A harp was playing in the distant corner, the woman who played it was dressed in a white silk gown that flowed with such ease, it looked like an upscale toga. The ring of ivy in her hair lent itself well to the dreamy image of something so pure and so distant she might even be an angel.

Over the sound of the harp, Jack could hear the conversations buzzing. "Who is the new neighbor?" he heard one woman say with enthusiastic curiosity. "This party is not for her is it, because I think she's been here awhile. I think instead it's for the new guy who moved in more recently, two houses down."

Her friend responded, "You mean that hunk of a man who sometimes comes out onto his balcony, shirtless, after sweating on that treadmill you can see in his front window?"

"Yes, I think that's who this party is for."

The friend squeeled, "Oh, I hope he's here. I'd sure like to meet him."

"Meet who?" a man said, who walked up to the two gossiping women.

"Oh, no one dear," the lady quickly changed the subject then gave her husband a peck on the lips.

Jack's cheeks reddened slightly. Although he was used to being admired by women, he was not quite that comfortable hearing such girl talk about himself. He made his way through the room smiling politely and headed towards the bar where the champagne was being poured. He sought refuge behind his glass and stood quietly at the bar where he could observe the occupants in the room.

Jack thought it a pity that only the homeowners were invited and that staff could not be present. His goal was to present himself as bait for more of the crime ring's minions in order to draw closer to their leader. Just as Jack began to wonder if his time was being wasted, his attention was drawn to the top of an elegant winding stair case, with double sets of stairs that met at a center, which was emphasized by a rounded balcony fit for a princess to waive to her subjects below.

The white marble stairs were starkly contrasted against the intricately woven black iron railings. The black and white setting drew one's eyes up to a pop of color on the center balcony, of the richest, deepest royal blue, which perfectly hugged the body of the woman who wore it—the same dress, now in color, of the woman in the silhouette on the champagne bottle, Jack had received with his invitation. The brightly lit crystal chandelier hanging directly above the balcony, upon which she stood, made the diamonds adorning her neck, twisting on her wrist, and dangling from her ears, sparkle. The slight and gentle movement of her hand on the railing, and the subtle twist of her body towards Jack's direction, made the cascade of light dazzle even more spectacularly.

The dazzling movement of her body gave Jack a direct view of her plunging neckline, which exposed the top half of her breasts, while still appropriately covering enough of her bosom to make sex appeal remain dignified. Her tiny waist was perfectly framed between her soft-looking voluptuous breasts and her teasingly round hips. The dress was long. It was down to her feet. But the slit along her left leg reached the top of her thigh. High but narrow, the slit in her dress teased a man with the promise that more skin lie beneath. As Jack gazed up at her, one word came to mind: *Venus.* It was the goddess, Venus, incarnate—brought to life by the Greco-Roman harpist playing sweet music.

In the dazzling light beneath which she stood, even from that great distance, Jack could see captivating stark blue eyes.

When her eyes met his, Venus' heart skipped a beat. Surprised by the strange feeling, her mouth opened slightly, as she caught her breath. Jack's mouth subconsciously opened in response, as if ready to receive her kiss.

Venus slowly began her descent down the marble stairs and Jack watched as her hips swung naturally with every step she took. Her movement was gracious, feminine, delicate. It made Jack fully aware of his masculinity. He subconsciously walked towards her and reached out his hand to help her down the last step.

Looking deep into his brown eyes, Venus whispered a breathy, "Thank you," and Jack smiled wide, raising his shoulders upwards and back, ever so slightly, making his strong chest puff out just a little more. Hand in hand he walked Venus toward the crowd, where he allowed her to lead the conversation.

When she spoke, her voice was just as much of a treat as her appearance. The most perfect English accent came out, as she said: "Neighbors and friends, allow me to introduce to you, the guest of honor, Mr. Jack Smith."

The party guests gathered around the two of them, as polite greetings were made, questions were asked, appropriate jokes were told, and laughter and gaiety filled the room. As the party went on, the handsome new couple remained side by side. It must have been an hour later that Jack realized he was still holding her soft, delicate hand. He clasped it a little tighter, not wanting to let go. She stood by his side for the duration of the party, as Jack forgot all about the reason he was in Bel Air.

As the evening grew later and the champagne relaxed him further, Jack turned to face the goddess by his side and realized he had not even asked her name. Still a stranger, but oh so close to him, he knew he needed to know this woman more. The knowledge he craved was overwhelmingly carnal. He scolded himself, ashamed of how ungentlemanly his thoughts were of such a fine, fine lady.

When the evening came to a close, Jack lifted Venus' hand to his lips and pressed them softly against her hand in a long indulgent kiss. Not wanting to pull away from the feel of her skin, he turned his cheek in a gentle caress against her hand when he turned his lips away and reluctantly released her hand.

The sensation caused Venus' eyes to widen, her heart to race and her breathing to subtly change to short deep breaths. Never had she felt such a strong desire to fall into bed with a man and lose herself completely to him, forgetting all her senses, and throwing caution completely to the wind. What a shame she thought it was, that he had to be *such a damned gentleman!*

"Until we meet again, my lady," Jack said, gallantly, excusing himself from her presence.

Disappointment gripping her, Venus sighed deeply, "Until we meet, again, Mr. Smith."

***

The next day, Jack sat at his dinning room table debriefing Gil on the few things he learned from the neighbors the prior evening. Despite the distraction of Venus, he had managed to drop a few questions asking for recommendations to help him staff his lifestyle. "Oh, just have your assistant call my assistant," was the most common answer he received. But he did manage to get addresses and calling cards so that he could send his assistant over to their homes to meet their staff and collect recommendations.

Jack instructed Gil to visit every home in the neighborhood and to get chatty with each assistant, looking for any signs that either they or the people they were recommending were part of the crime ring. He told him to drop hints that would make a predator believe Jack was easy prey.

"Now, make sure you say things like: 'My boss is really generous;' 'He gives me carte blanche authority with his credit card,' 'He signs the bill at a restaurant without even looking to see how much it cost.' Things like that."

Gil agreed those were good one-line baiters. He then stated the obvious, which he hoped would be true: "Fishing this way is going to take a long time. It could take us years to infiltrate this crime ring. I'm not complaining though, I could really get used to this lifestyle!"

"Well don't," Jack advised, "We don't have years. We only have a few months."

"Why!" complained Gil, "all my undercover jobs take years!"

"Yeah, but none of those are as expensive as this one. I was only able to cajole your bosses and mine for a certain fixed budget to spend on this case. They all unequivocally told me that when the money runs out, the investigation ends. We arrest all the minions we find, but if the ringleader is not discovered, that's too bad."

"Then, we're going to need reinforcements."

"You're all I got. And the only reason they assigned you is because you were due for a vacation after that huge take down you just finished, and they figured this would be as good as a vacation."

"I sure can't complain," Gil agreed.

"Yeah, but I still need more support. I'll see what strings I can pull."

Just then the doorbell rang and Jack stood to answer it. Gil put his hand up and said, "Now, *this* door, I think I am supposed to answer."

"Oh yes, of course. Go ahead," said Jack as he sat back down.

When Gil opened the door, Jack heard that sultry, most perfect English accent from the prior evening. He bolted out of his chair and walked quickly towards the sound of her voice.

This morning, she was dressed in the most innocent and precious looking summer dress. It was white with flowers and capped sleeves that were delicately ruffled. The neckline was high, but her large bust could still be appreciated by the shape of the dress, which hugged her trim waist. Not too tight and not too loose, it went down past her knees with a 1950s style flare from below the waist line, which added sweet innocence to her natural sex appeal.

When Jack made his way to the door, he whispered to Gil to get lost for several hours. He then greeted this unnamed beauty and asked her to join him in his living room. She came bearing fresh baked goods, which she claimed to have baked herself. Jack's heart melted, becoming even more invested at the sight of such innocence and nurturing care starkly contrasted against the Venus who had come down the stairs the night before—a vivid image which had burned itself into his memory.

"Please, come sit down, make yourself comfortable," he said.

"Oh thank you, I would love to," she beamed cheerfully.

When Jack heard the door close behind Gil, followed by the engine of the Lamborghini revving to life, he sat close enough to Venus that his leg touched hers. He put his arm on the edge of the couch behind her back and turned his torso slightly to face her. She cast sweet eyes up at his and waited for him to speak.

"Forgive me," Jack apologized. "The party you threw in my honor last night was so captivating and so mesmerizing, that I forgot to even ask your name."

"It's Victoria," she lied.

"Well that's very fitting," Jack replied, "It's a name fit for a queen."

"Yes, indeed," Venus said, "The name of my ancestress, actually." Then Venus charmed Jack with the life story of the persona she always used while in the United States. Being the descendent of an illegitimate child of one of Queen Victoria's sons never failed to dazzle an American. She had told the story so many times by now, that it was as much a part of her as if it were true. Because it felt like the truth to Venus, when she told the story, even Jack's very sharp and experienced prosecutorial mind was not alerted to any signs of fraud. He was as dazzled by her this morning, as he was attracted to her last night; and now, she intrigued him with her charm, her wit, her intelligence. Every single thing about her was as perfect as any woman could be.

Jack watched this delicate beauty, so well mannered and proper, so refined, with so much elegance holding back such strong sex appeal, that he couldn't help but think, "who is this goddess I've found?"

Then, just as if she had read his mind, she said, "But I prefer to be called 'Venus.' That is my middle name."

Of course, it wasn't her middle name. It was the only real first name she ever had. She couldn't bear to have him call her by any other name. If she were going to make love to this man—and she had every intention of doing so—she wanted him to call out her real name in the throes of passion—and she had every intention of bringing him there—but not just yet. First, she had to drive him mad with desire.

Venus stood, and with a sweet voice said, "I must go."

Jack stood too. Then, he bent forward slightly to pick up her hand, as he gave it a gentle kiss before walking her to the door.

She very graciously accepted every bit of his chivalry.

CHAPTER 10

He was only 57, but because he had started his job at such a young age, he was already retired. He was still physically fit, a large man with broad shoulders, 6'0" tall with dark hair and pale blue eyes. The lines on his face did not make him look old. They made him look accomplished, distinguished and learned. And he was.

Today, he sat in a room inside his home, which his friends had dubbed "the man cave of all man caves." His cigar lay burning in the ashtray beside his favorite, brown leather arm chair, nearly forgotten as he pondered how he should answer the next question on the registration form. He was signing up to attend an international conference, which would be attended by the most distinguished private investigators, detectives and leading law enforcement officers from agencies throughout the United States and Europe. He had attended the conference every year for the past 10 years. It was a good way to keep his knowledge sharp, as the conference covered the latest in scientific forensic testing, the challenges defense attorneys were making to such tests, and what law enforcement could do to anticipate and prepare for such challenges. The fun part of the conference was when the most wanted profiles were presented and leading officers would gather and exchange information to see if an elusive criminal was leaving traces of his crimes in different jurisdictions. Once it had been noticed that many a cold case had been solved by officers from different jurisdictions discussing their cold cases over beers in the evenings after lectures and classes had concluded, the conference decided to add a formal program to the conference dedicated to allowing a panel of officers from different jurisdictions to present their most interesting and/or elusive criminals on their most wanted lists.

As he sat in his soft, worn down, leather armchair, he pondered whether he wanted to answer "retired" in response to the question "occupation" or if he should answer: "private investigator." If he answered "private investigator," that might cause his phone to ring even more often than it already did. His two main clients, Jack Wayne and Sarah Cartwright, were already keeping him busier than he wanted to be. His "part time" work as a P.I., was only meant to keep him from getting too bored in retirement; but recently, it had kept him busier than the days he was still working as a lead detective on the police force.

Sarah had now begun her career as a historian and author, and she frequently needed him to research archives, official records in various jurisdictions and even to travel to far off destinations in order to interview the descendants of famous historical figures. She insisted on chasing down the finest details so that when she wrote a historical fiction novel, it would keep an element of truth running throughout the book. Occasionally, she would send him off to fact check a news anchor or political pundit so that she could skewer them on her blog whenever they spewed something untruthful. She was ruthless when she did this. Always the pursuer of truth and justice, Sarah Cartwright was as demanding of him on these projects as she had been when she worked as a prosecutor leading major crime teams to solve cases and bring the offender to justice.

The retired detective picked up his cigar now and drew in a deep puff as he glared at the registration form in his hand, empty only where the form asked: "occupation."

Then the phone rang.

He picked it up and said hello, only to hear a familiar voice proceed with its demands without introduction:

"One more thing, Detective . . ."

"That's not my name anymore," he quipped.

"Well, you're still the best one I've got," answered Jack Wayne.

"Fine," said Detective Jones, as he pressed the end of his cigar into the ashtray, putting it out. He would not spoil the joys of retirement while accepting more never ending detective work.

Jack Wayne proceeded with his demands: "This one is a white collar crime case. I have a banker who won't give me the identities of the victims without a subpoena. So I need you to pay him a visit to pump him for information, without him realizing what he's divulging to you. I need to know where the victims live and who's on their payroll, so we can infiltrate their staff."

"No problem," said Detective Jones, "What information do you have so far."

"So far, I have reports of suspicious activity appearing in their bank accounts, without any names or account numbers. Just go in there and chat up the banker. Get him talking about why he suspects these transactions. That should loosen him up enough to spill details without realizing it. He might give you enough to piece together and identify households that I need to target."

"I'm on it," answered Detective Jones.

CHAPTER 11

Gil sat at a shared desk with the personal assistant of Jack's new drinking partner. The millionaire Jack had recently befriended took to him quickly. They'd had a lively political debate at the country club where nobody else would indulge Fred Herman in such arguments. To him, Jack was a fresh face who was an even fresher breath of air. When Fred Herman began drinking and bellowing about the wrong direction the US was headed in, the other members of the country club would slowly move away from him, not wanting to ruffle the wrong feathers. It was their polite custom to never talk politics. But Fred hated that. So when Jack Wayne challenged Fred one day at the bar, with his own analysis, they became fast friends.

Today, they were playing pool in Fred's billiards room. While there, Jack had asked if Fred wouldn't mind the imposition of Jack's personal assistant coming over so that Jack could take a quick peek at some papers before signing. "Of course! Of course!" Fred had bellowed, "My Casa is Your Casa," he misstated. "If you need him to print anything, just use my office upstairs where my assistant can help him out." At that, Jack capitalized on the opportunity to bring Gil over to interact with one of the women who Detective Jones had identified as a potential suspect in the crime ring. Even more fortuitously, Jack had no idea how much his previous decision to cave-in to Gil's persistent request for a Lamborghini would now serve to draw this vulture out of her nest.

***

As Gil sat at the desk typing a fake email to nobody in particular, Fred's assistant, Beth, was staring out the window at a shiny object glistening in the sun, which kept her transfixed.

"Wow!" she exclaimed, "How do you drive a car like that, if you're only his personal assistant!"

"It's not mine. It's his. If I ever get canned, I lose the car. That's why I jump when he snaps his fingers."

"Doesn't it suck to be this close to wealth, but not really be a part of it?"

"Yeah, but it beats operating heavy machinery or moving heavy boxes."

"I sometimes hate them so much, I wonder if I'd rather do that instead."

"Who? Your bosses?"

"Yeah, why should they have all this? They don't even appreciate it. They can't even imagine what it's like to have to work for a living."

"Would you really quit? Does your boss not give you any perks like mine does?"

"Only if I take the perks myself."

Beth's response kicked Gil's undercover skills into overdrive. He quickly seized on the moment that every undercover agent looks for. It is the moment his target first hints at criminal intent, the moment he can prove himself equally criminally minded. Gil answered Beth with an intrigue filled voice, as he smoothly said: "Oooh, that sounds like something I'd like to learn more about."

Beth smiled coyley and said, "Only my closest friends learn my secrets."

"Well then, lets get close," Gill suggested, "Maybe even closer than friends," he charmed, as he leaned in, pausing momentarily to look into her eyes before dazzling her with his dimple-blessed smile. When her face brightened with wide eyes and an even wider grin, Gil leaned in for the kiss.

Beth was not the most attractive woman a man might encounter. She was slightly overweight by L.A. standards, which meant she was between a size 10 and 12. She had short brown hair that remained frizzy despite being washed and combed. She never wore makeup, and generally speaking, had the appearance of someone who had long since given up on trying to be beautiful. But she shouldn't have. Her facial features were quite pretty. Had she put a little more effort into self-presentation, she could have been quite attractive to the opposite sex. However, due to her bad habit of lack of self-care, she was not competitive on the L.A. dating scene. She didn't turn heads, and it was rare that she attracted male attention. This was the reason Gil's kiss had such an impact on her. She couldn't believe such a gorgeous man wanted to kiss her. Desperate for more, Beth put her hand on his leg and moved it up his thigh.

Gil caught her hand and stopped her. She became embarrassed, pulled away from his kiss and turned away. "Uh, um, I'm sorry, I'm so sorry," she began apologizing profusely.

"No, don't be," Gil said gently, lifting his hand and turning her chin towards him. He kissed her lips with a quick peck, then explained, "It's just that my boss is downstairs."

Hope returned to Beth's face when she heard this excuse.

Gil then offered her even more promise, "Let's pick this up another time. When are you off of work for a day?

"Sunday!" Beth offered enthusiastically.

"Heeeyyy," Gil said smoothly, "So am I."

CHAPTER 12

Gil lie lazily in Beth's studio apartment in the wrong part of Hollywood. It was a dingy dilapidated building run by a slumlord who had been cited by the city for various health and safety violations. This was the third consecutive Sunday Gil spent there with Beth, and she was already calling him her boyfriend. Strategically, he never corrected her.

He was in the bed, which doubled as a couch, and Beth was standing at the kitchenette. She promised him that whipped cream would make their exchange that much more sexy and fun. However, Gil's mind was on work not fun. He had to get her to start talking. He couldn't just spend the entire day in bed. He hoped that the strawberry Margaritas she had so proudly served him, as part of their brunch-in-bed date, would loosen her lips.

When she came back to the bed, Gil gently took the bottle of whipped cream out of her hands and pulled her in for a kiss. Holding her with one arm, he placed the whipped cream on the night stand at the opposite side of the bed. Then he wrapped both arms around her and gently moved her beneath him. As she lie there expectantly, he stared into her eyes. She sighed. Then he nestled in close to her, making himself comfortable, while keeping her firmly in his arms. "Let's just snuggle," he said, "I like snuggling." Beth laughed, but Gil didn't care. He had a job to do.

Gil ran his fingers through her hair and gently kissed the left side of her face. Then he whispered in her ear, "So, tell me more about how to get rich quick."

Beth's eyes got big and she smiled broadly, even more excited about the thought of financial gain than she had been about anticipated sex. Gil waited patiently for Beth's greediness and arrogance to take over.

To nudge her along, Gil pressed his lips to Beth's ear, "Get me hot. The thought of money makes me hot."

"Me too!" Beth squealed.

"Then tell me," he whispered, his hot breath into her ear, "How do you and I get rich quick?"

"You and I?" Beth asked hopefully.

"Yeah, teach me what you know, so I'll have extra cash to spend on you."

Gil's promise pushed Beth's greed into highspeed. More for him, meant more for her. Unwittingly, she began her confession: "Well, instead of 'Charlie's Angels, we're more like "Charlotte's Angels."

"What's that supposed to mean?" Gil asked.

"It means we're the opposite of Charlie's Angeles. We're so opposite that it's even a lady on the phone who gives us orders, not a man."

"Her name is Charlotte?"

"No, we call her that because nobody knows who she really is. It's just a disembodied voice from a different untraceable number, each time she calls."

"So, why do you follow her instructions?"

"Because, whenever I perform the small task she asks me to, later I find an envelope of cash, dressed up as junk mail, in my mailbox."

"How much cash is it, usually?"

"It depends on what I've done for her. Like that time I booked everyone for a trip to Aspen that none of our bosses went on, I got a lot of money for that. I got like a thousand dollars!"

"Aspen?" Gil asked, "That sounds fun. You all got to go to Aspen without your bosses?"

"I wouldn't say 'we got to,' that's one of those moments I took a perk that my boss would never give me on his own. So, there's that too. It's not just the envelopes of cash. She helps us live the lifestyle as if we were our bosses, and not just their lowly staff."

"So, how does it work?"

"I don't really know how it works. At first, when she had us double booking stuff, I thought she worked for the hotel or airline or whatever. But then I noticed we were instructed to double book and over charge everything, from all different businesses and places."

"Don't your bosses become suspicious?"

"No. They never notice. That's why I'm telling you they don't deserve all that money. They don't even care if a $700 per night hotel room is charged twice for the same day."

"So, I don't get it. If she's not working for a specific company, why the double bookings?"

"I don't know. We're not supposed to ask any questions, or even talk to each other about this. But I think it has something to do with the refunds. We're supposed to double delete the emails and shred any letters that come in from the businesses confirming that a booking was refunded. I started noticing that the refund never shows up on the credit card account that was used for the double booking."

"You have access to your boss' credit card statements?"

"Only the ones he gives me to book stuff with."

"What else do you do for Charlotte?"

"Well, whenever my boss gets a new credit card or debit card, I have to fax both sides of it and the statements that go with it to a fax number she gives me."

"Do you ever draw cash from those cards and pocket it?"

"I can't pocket it. If I want to continue getting money, I have to put it all in an outgoing envelope that I place in a mailbox she tells me to use on a specific day and time, with the red flag raised. Later, I get my share in my mailbox."

"Why do you settle for less, if you're the one sticking your neck out?"

"Because, we saw a girl go to jail for a really long time for trying to keep the money herself. As long as we obey orders, we keep getting cash in our mailboxes. But the minute anyone tries to do it themselves, boom! Their bosses suddenly discover what they've done, with all kinds of paper evidence piled up proving their guilt."

"Did that girl ever try to identify Charlotte? You know, like you sometimes see on those cop shows on tv, if you give up the ringleader, you go free?"

"She tried, but everyone thought she was making it up. She actually got ridiculed pretty badly for it. I overheard her former bosses laughing about it at a party once, when they were asking their friends for recommendations for a new assistant. They mocked her: 'A strange voice, coming out of nowhere on the phone,' They thought it was one of the dumbest stories a criminal could make up."

"Well," asked Gil, "didn't she give them a phone number she used to communicate with Charlotte?"

"We're not allowed to call Charlotte unless it's an emergency so bad that only she can handle it. Like if we don't know how to respond to a fraud alert from a bank—but that rarely happens."

"What phone number do you call?"

"Only Angels who've been with her a long time get an emergency number for trying to reach her. If you reach that level, you get your own number to use, but she changes it often. Anyway, we learned through the mistake of the fallen Angel that the emergency number Charlotte gives us will trace back to us. In her case, she gave the police the phone number she supposedly used to text Charlotte. But the police found that it was a pre-paid disposable phone, opened under her own name, using her boss' credit card. That kind of sealed her coffin on top of all the other evidence."

"What was the other evidence against the fallen Angel?"

"All the unauthorized credit card charges were made from her computer, and when she withdrew cash out of the ATM, the video on the ATM captured her face. So, there was no way out for her. Also, somehow her name was on a bank account that the refunds the police were investigating went into. I don't know how that happened. Rumor has it that she didn't know how it happened either. The police asked her to identify the people working with her. They thought she had to know someone on the inside from the business that refunded the money to her account instead of the card that was charged, but she couldn't do that either. That's why she went to jail for so long. It looked like she refused to cooperate with the police."

"So, how do you ever quit working for Charlotte, if you want to?"

"You don't. Once you've done it once, you're Charlotte's Angel for life."

"Sounds a little scary, but exciting. How do I become one of Charlotte's Angels?"

Beth smiled at him hesitantly. Despite all the alcohol she'd indulged in that lazy Sunday, awareness began to flood her mind. She was now kicking herself for having answered all his questions. Due to the alcohol, and Gil's charm, she belatedly realized that she had been admitting to someone she barely knew that she is an active participant in a crime ring. Suddenly realizing that she had said too much, Beth decided that the best course of action would be to ensnare Gil too, so that he couldn't rat her out. Her answer was smooth: "Just tell me the address you want to receive your envelopes of cash.

I have your phone number already. I'll just write your number and address on a card I place in my next cash drop, and you'll be in!"

"Just like that?"

"Yeah. She only uses people smart enough to understand her code. You will have to wait several weeks. Then you'll get a strange call from a woman who doesn't speak in full sentences. She'll call you no more than three times repeating the same code. If you obey the orders in the code, you're in. If not, you're out.

CHAPTER 13

When the delivery driver put the groceries in his vehicle bound for 944 Bel Air Way, he slipped a small sealed envelope, containing an index card, into one of the bags, and dutifully drove to the house that had just pinged his app for grocery deliveries. If he had not managed to be the first driver to accept the request from this address, he would be required to accept the next order it made the same day. Otherwise, he would lose his lucrative position as the favorite driver who delivered to this address. The address ordered groceries daily, but only occasionally received a special envelope. Today, the delivery driver caught the grocery order on the first ping. That usually meant a better tip.

Fifteen minutes later, he handed the groceries to the beautiful woman who answered the door, and she handed him a $100 bill. Her long, blonde wig and oversized sunglasses disguised her face. A shade of lipstick, she'd never dare wear under any other circumstance, provided additional distraction and cover. The overcoat, which was three sizes too big for her, masked her physique. The delivery driver thought she looked like the perfect cliché of a kept mistress—an assumption he made from the heart-shaped sticker on the outside of the envelope, which always served as his clue telling him which address the envelope was bound for.

Upon receiving his $100 tip, the delivery driver left happy. He assumed the secret message, which he never dared open, was from a married man who'd found a much safer and smarter way of texting his mistress. He skipped down the front steps believing forbidden love was more lucrative than his other deliveries.

A few minutes later, Venus removed her wig and overcoat, and wiped off the hideous lipstick. She pulled the index card from the envelope, and dialed the number written on it. When she heard the young man answer, she spoke quickly: "Fax. 325 Switzerland 8973." Then she hung up.

Two houses down the road, Gil looked up at Jack, "Did they get that!"

"What?" asked Jack.

"That call. Did they put the trace on my phone yet?"

"Should have, I told them to."

"I need the trace on that call I just got!" exclaimed Gil.

"Impossible!" Jack insisted. "Far too short of a call. Was that her? What'd she say?"

Gil wrote the numbers down on his notepad before he forgot them. "This is all she said: 'Fax. 325 Switzerland 8973.'

"Ok," Jack remarked, "That's an easy one. She wants you to fax something to that fax number in Switzerland. We just need to look up the country code for Switzerland, and we'll have all the numbers we need to send the fax. What does she want you to fax?"

Overly excited over the fact that Charlotte took the bait—something he never thought would be so easy—Gil stumbled over his words. "Ummm, uh," he snapped his fingers repeatedly, as if trying to remember something, "Statements! She wants bank statements! Credit card statements! Anything she can use to steal from, if we just give her the opportunity!"

"Oh, that's perfect," Jack said, "We'll give her the statements then track them more closely than our uninterested victims do, and soon the transactions we see will lead us right to her!"

Jack patted Gil on the back. "Well done, Gil. Excellent job!"

CHAPTER 14

Over the next thirty days, Jack's strategy was to wait; but while he and Gil waited, they were enjoying life tremendously.

Gil, in particular, was having the time of his life. He had been spending like a billionaire on the dummy account Jack had set up under a company named JAK LLC. It was generously funded by money seized from drug dealers and forfeited to the state. Because this was not the type of job that would warrant creating a false social security number with which a bank account could be created in Jack's false name, Jack settled for creating a limited liability company used by his billionaire persona to hold an expense account to which his personal assistant, Gil, had free reign and access. The debit card connected to the JAK LLC expense account would be used to make lavish purchases and book expensive services. Gil was now enjoying every bit of that spending spree.

Because he and Jack had not yet pinpointed which businesses "Charlotte" cooperates with to misdirect refunds, Jack instructed Gil to shop, shop, shop and spend, spend, spend at all the best locations in Beverly Hills, Hollywood, and Malibu. Gil would have steak and lobster in Beverly Hills one night, then sushi in Malibu the next night. He booked $300 massages at one luxury spa and hotel one day, then another the next day. But he wasn't going to let this high living go to waste. He invited some of the most beautiful women he was meeting at the Hollywood clubs he was now frequenting to keep him company. These clubs were buzzing with gorgeous models and wannabe actresses hoping to brush elbows with a famous movie producer who might give them their next gig. Each of these beautiful women were also all too eager to spend time with an attractive young man who had access to a seemingly limitless expense account.

It was Gil's job to make the bank statement he would be faxing to "Charlotte" in Switzerland, look like that of a billionaire new to L.A. With multiple dinners, multiple massages and multiple hotel rooms purchased on the same evening, this bank statement would make JAK LLC look like an easy target.

Tonight, Gil was at the opening of the newest Hollywood club, complete with "A" list actors, red carpet and paparazzi. He was already inside before the celebrities began showing up. The expense account had purchased him the privilege to sit at a VIP table in the newest and most exclusive club. It cost a mere $4,000 just for the privilege of sitting there that evening. The table was round, with a semi-circle shaped booth for seating, which was made of lush, comfortable velvet. It was a rich color purple that appeared to change to blue whenever the dim lights changed color with the loud music that vibrated all around. Gil sat in the middle of the booth, surrounded by the many different models and wannabe actresses he had met on prior evenings. He looked around at the women at his table, with a beaming grin more dazzling than the champagne bottle that had been lit with a sparkler, which was now being brought to his table by an even more attractive woman than the ones seated beside him. "Hi there," Gil greeted the beautiful waitress, whose boots came up to her thighs, a few inches lower than her tight skirt. The waitress smiled and placed the champagne on his table. She made eye contact with him but walked away quickly, as if to say, come chase me. Gil's eyes chased. The redhead sitting beside him stroked his arm, and he turned to give her a quick kiss, still not forgetting the beautiful waitress who had just walked away. The brunette with the big green eyes sitting to his left reached for the bottle and said: "Come on! Let's party!" Gil placed his arms around each of them and, still smiling, shouted: "Pour!"

***

While Gil had been gallivanting the best parts of Hollywood, Beverly Hills and Malibu, Jack had been falling deeper and deeper into the web of love, spun by Venus—the woman he believed was named Victoria. From that electrifying moment he had first seen her, his passion and desire for her grew more and more intense. Not only was this the most magnificently beautiful woman he had ever seen, but she was smart, and funny, and worldly, and classy, and elegant; yet, somehow, she was also the most warm and lovely homemaker he had ever encountered. It seemed unreal to him that a woman could be all that. In his past, Jack felt he had to choose between a woman who was either, a warm, loving and caring homemaker; or a woman who was a smart, sophisticated, career woman. This was part of the reason it never crossed his mind to marry Jillian. While Jillian had everything he could want in terms of personality, she simply never conjured up images of a wife and mother. Lacking that effect on a man, Jillian simply never triggered Jack's instincts. Her status in his heart had never elevated beyond him merely enjoying Jillian as the most likely person he'd spend his free time with. If she had pushed the topic, Jillian would certainly have won the most suitable mate contest, and would have ultimately become his wife, one day. However, the instinct within Jack never arose in a way that would compel him to pursue her for marriage, on his own volition.

In contrast, Venus knew how to play on every instinct within a man. She understood that beauty, seduction and charm were only lures for initial attraction. She could use these characteristics for temporary distraction, or to dazzle a man out of his mind momentarily; but to capture a man to keep as her own, Venus knew she had to lavish him with a display of love and care in the style of a 1950s housewife; and when she chose to, Venus would seamlessly transition into the kind of woman who might say: "the best way to a man's heart, is through his stomach." In this way that she carefully mixed the old world with the modern world, there was not a man on earth who could escape Venus' prowess if he became her target. Since the day she saw him glimmering in the sun, on his Bel Air balcony, Jack had been Venus' target.

What Venus hadn't bargained for, however, was that she too would be falling in love with him. The stolen blue Bugatti she had left out in the open for far too long, was now parked in Jack's driveway, next to his. A mistake she would never make, if in her right mind. But as much as she captivated Jack, he captivated her; and Venus continued throwing caution to the wind. She couldn't send the car off now, because it still had new license plates. Jack had already noticed it was a new purchase and commented on it, asking her how she liked her new car. For the car to disappear suddenly would only arouse suspicion or questions she didn't feel like answering. She was also enjoying Jack's company far too much to leave him now. So she stayed in L.A. longer than she should have, and she left the blue Bugatti out in the open, still confident that it could be explained as a civil matter, if the dealership ever caught up to her. She was careful not to drive it outside the gates of their Bel Air community, as an added precaution. In any event, the car dealership would be looking for a woman named Katherine, who lived in Orange County, not a woman named Victoria who lived in Bel Air. Therefore, Venus calculated that as long as the stolen Bugatti never left her gated community in Bel Air, she would never be found by the angry dealership. More so than this strategic calculation, her out of character conduct was also driven by the fact that Jack was well worth the risk, making him, and the pursuit of him, all that much more thrilling.

Now, Venus was snuggling up to Jack on the couch when the doorbell rang. He excused himself to answer the door. As he did this, Venus walked to the window to peer out over the sunlit hills of California. A man driving a UPS truck, and wearing a UPS uniform handed Jack a package. As he walked back to his truck, he saw Venus' face in the window, but she did not notice him. He mumbled under his breath, "Jack, you lucky dog, you." Then, Detective Jones reentered the borrowed UPS truck to get it back to the real driver, who on many occasions, had allowed Detective Jones to use it to deliver documents without detection. The package contained additional information uncovered by Detective Jones, including more detail about the fallen pawn Beth described to Gil, as well as a long list of the pawns who had already been identified as potential participants in the crime ring. Before walking back to the living room, Jack placed the package in a safe under a desk in the den. He hurried back to the living room, eager for more of Venus' love.

He found her standing in the window, showered in sunlight. It was a sight to behold. Her posture was perfect. Her dress was elegant, but sexy. It wrapped itself tightly around her feminine curves. She had one hand on her hip, which accentuated the perfect ratio between her waist and her hips. Her waist was tiny, but her hips gave a man something to grab and pull towards him. Her legs were long, and her tall torso seemed to offer a man's eyes more to behold of the exquisite beauty that was Venus.

Jack approached her from behind, placing his hands on her hips, while his lips gently met her neck. She rewarded him with a delicate sigh that told him she welcomed his touch. Then suddenly she turned to embrace him, grabbing him tight, pulling him towards her and pressing her lips against his, hard with a passionate French kiss. Her raw feminine power excited Jack to heights previously unknown to him. The kiss was the kiss of woman that said you are mine, you shall be mine, and I shall be yours. It was passionate and enduring and thrilling. Jack's body begged for more.

He reluctantly pulled his mouth away so that he could speak. He pressed his lips into her ear and begged breathlessly, "Venus, come upstairs with me." She grabbed his chin with her left hand and forced his mouth back to hers for more of that passionate kiss that neither of them wanted to let go. Finally, she breathed her answer, "Yes, Jack, Yes!" The two of them hurried up the stairs together, hand in hand. Upon reaching Jack's bedroom, they collapsed on top of Jack's soft bed, entangled, as they tumbled and rolled and kissed and grabbed, in passionate fury.

Finally, ... finally, they could *make love*. After thirty long days they'd spent together, each and every day, spending quality time, engaging in enchanting conversation, indulging in fine wine and finer meals, enjoying sweet affection, but never sex. Finally! They were making love. And they made love, over and over and over again, until night fell and morning came.

***

When Jack awoke late the next morning, Venus lie sleeping beside him. He turned his head and gazed lovingly into her face. He soaked up the calm and quite of the moment, as he indulged in the sight of his precious beauty. As he gazed upon this woman, Jack still felt the powerful emotions she evoked in him the night before—happiness, fulfillment, pure satisfaction. Most powerful of all was the overwhelming thrill of everything Venus embodied: a perfect lady—sweet, precious, delicate; but, also a vixen—hot, passionate and thrilling, and all of those things at once, and each of those things at just the right moments. Jack had never met anyone like Venus. As he watched his sleeping beauty, Jack pressed his lips against her cheek with a soft kiss, then he whispered a silent vow into her ear, as she slept peacefully, beautifully. Jack vowed that one day he would make Venus his wife.

CHAPTER 15

Venus stood in her walk-in-closet, which was larger than most people's master bedrooms. Behind a thick collection of Versace dresses, was a secret door. She slid the dresses to one side and pushed a button, which looked like one of the decorative rhinestones that framed the back wall. When a portion of the wall slid open, she quickly stepped inside the hidden room and the sliding wall snapped shut behind her. This was her office. It was a 1000 square foot rectangle hidden between the exterior wall and the back closet walls of adjoining rooms. It had only one entrance, and no windows, using only four inch vents near the ceiling, lining the exterior wall for ventilation. In this room, were file drawers full of the bank statements of her most active files. These files contained all the information she needed to keep her income stream steady. They told her the purchasing patterns of her pawns' employers. In her mind, she would refer to these victims as her "clients."

In a different set of drawers, Venus kept hundreds of old burner phones (none of which were smart phones) that she had accumulated over many years. She never gave an instruction more than once from the same phone. Each phone would be disposed of after each use. That is why a small pizza oven was also located in this secret room. It could cook pizza at 800 degrees, or melt a burner phone faster than it could ever be tracked. Because she might spend hours in this room, studying transactions and strategizing her next move, Venus also decorated the room with pleasantries. On the far wall opposite the entrance, was an interior waterfall. In the middle of the room, facing the waterfall was a comfortable but elegant writing desk, and rolling arm chair. Within a few steps to the right of that was a small glass door wine cooler filled with her favorite wines and champagne, which sat beneath a counter boasting the most high tech instant cappuccino maker. In a second wine cooler, she stored bottles of water. Because she would sometimes meditate to the sound of the waterfall, she also kept a chaise lounge in the corner near the waterfall, so she could lie against its arm, place her feet up and watch the waterfall.

But this room was meant for work, not meditation. An old-fashioned land line fax machine was also located in this room. Only one person in the world new this fax number. It was her partner overseas, who would fax the bank statements to her, after receiving them from a pawn. He would change his location as Venus changed her location, never receiving a fax in the same jurisdiction Venus was in.

When she first created this room, she had determined that this house in Bel Air was the best place to keep such a room. It was the only item present in her lifestyle that wasn't stolen property.

The house had been deeded to her by a man in Monaco who had lost a game of poker to her. Dazzled by her beauty, and drunk off expensive scotch, he had very inappropriately challenged her to a poker game, to gamble for one evening alone with her.

However, by the time the Scotch had grown his courage enough to make the indecent proposal, Venus had already identified several of his weaknesses. He was obesely overweight with a round face. In their short conversation leading up to his indecent proposal, he told Venus that he'd beaten the odds by living as long as he had, given his long history of gluttony and excess. He coughed as he had explained to her, that he wasn't surprised that the drugs hadn't killed him, but the alcohol and cigarettes certainly should have by now. Then he bellowed with laughter as if that were the funniest joke ever told. He further explained to her that he had long since given up trying to charm a woman, and confessed that this was now his way, admitting that it was a dishonorable way to live. He was the type of man who believed that openly accepting one's faults was the method for achieving excuse or forgiveness for bad behavior. Knowing that men like him were the easiest targets, Venus responded strategically. Instead of gasping in shock or scolding his obscene proposal, Venus countered him with poise and elegance, stating sweetly: "No thank you. That would be highly inappropriate." This, of course, had made her even more desirable to the man. He shuffled the cards, and bridged them between his hands as he looked at Venus with a devil's grin, while stating: "The fact that you didn't slap me, means there is hope!" Playing along, Venus had teased him and tantalized him for hours, while pouring him more and more to drink from the expensive bottle he had invited her to share with him in the VIP section of the casino in Monte Carlo, where he'd encountered her.

He had hoped to win an evening with her, but she refused to play for those stakes. She convinced him instead to play for other stakes. Owning many lavish properties around the world, he quickly offered up the deed to his house in Bel Air to bet against one evening alone with her. She somehow convinced him instead, to play for only one kiss, and that if she felt love in his kiss, she would spend more than an evening with him, perhaps a lifetime. At first, he told her he was too old to plan for the future, and that one guaranteed night offered him better odds than the hope of many more nights. However, Venus continued to charm him, as he continued to drink. Finally, he reached a point where he was so inebriated that he began to believe he was the one who had convinced her to raise the stakes by offering the potential of many nights with her. Thus, they played one hand of poker for one kiss from her, which she bet against one house from him. In the end, his straight flush was no match for her royal flush.

Today, Venus sat in her secret office, inside her legitimately owned Bel Air mansion, awaiting a fax from her partner. It had been approximately 35 days since the new potential pawn had responded to her instruction that he "Fax. 325 Switzerland 8973." She had deemed his response acceptable. It read: "Old statements already shredded, please await next statement cycle."

She now sat on her chaise lounge with a glass of champagne in her hand, as she watched the cascade of water fall before her eyes. She listened to the soothing sound of water falling as she thought of Jack Smith. She enjoyed him so much, she began to wonder whether she would ever retire from her life of crime, to make a long life with him. As her mind wandered down this road, she subconsciously shook the glass in her hand, rocking the contents inside it to the brim, though not spilling it. She thought of his smile, and his eyes, and his laughter; and she smiled too. She brought the champagne glass to her lips, tipping it gently, remembering his kiss, as the sweet liquid filled her mouth. "Jack," she whispered breathlessly after swallowing. The mere thought of him aroused her. She tilted her head back with laughter, thinking herself silly to react in such a way; but, her laughter was more than that, it was also filled with the joy she felt, just thinking of Jack Smith. For a moment, for one short moment, she wondered if she could trade in her current lifestyle to become the wife of Texas billionaire, Jack Smith.

The squeaking, screeching sound of an old fax machine firing up disrupted her thoughts. Venus jumped up with a start, nearly spilling the champagne. So deep in thoughts of Jack, she had almost forgotten she was awaiting the fax. She placed the glass down on a marble end table near the chaise lounge and walked over to the fax machine. She lifted six pages off of it and walked over to her desk. Her eyes widened and her mouth grinned with the excitement of seeing such a plump and easy new target. Looking back at the waterfall, which, only seconds ago, she had stared into wondering if she could give up her lifestyle for Jack, Venus shook her head and said out loud: "Not just yet, Jack, baby. Maybe later." The thrill of her game is what Venus couldn't resist. She just wasn't quite ready to give up her game.

CHAPTER 16

One hour later, Gil received his first instruction from Charlotte: "Add 1. All bookings."

He was both excited and dismayed. All bookings? Could she really be working with that many people around L.A.? He called Jack into the den from the dining room. "Hey, Jack! Jack! come in here for a minute!"

Jack came in and closed the door, "What's up?"

Gil answered, "Can you believe this? She wants me to add one to all bookings. What do you think that means? Does she really have someone on the inside at all these different businesses?"

"No, I don't think that's it."

"What could it be?"

"Well, she's probably just trying to confuse the account holder. Let's look at the bank statement, let's try to see her strategy."

As Gil and Jack reviewed the bank statement that Gil had faxed to Charlotte, they noticed a pattern Gil had not even noticed in his own spending. At each location, it was obvious that multiple people were at dinner, or getting a massage, or booking a hotel room at hotels that housed some of the most popular bars in the city.

Jack looked at Gil, "Did you even spend a single day alone over these past 30 days?"

Gil laughed.

"Gil, you know we're on a budget, don't you?"

"Yes, but, ..."

"I know, I know," Jack interrupted him, "It has to look like the spending of a man with such unlimited funds, he won't notice if some things are over-booked."

"Well, yeah that," said Gil, "and I also wanted to make it look like easy prey. With multiple charges already going on, how is a billionaire supposed to notice one more charge?"

"That's it!" Jack exclaimed. "She's playing a numbers game. If there is 1 extra booking on all bookings, it adds up. And it's completely undetectable to the account holder. How could he remember if he had 3 or 4 guests with him on a single night, when he has multiple guests, every night. Boy! she's strategic, isn't she? When the overbooking happens all over the place, it doesn't stick out like a sore thumb from the few places where she siphons the refunds—which makes it even harder for the account holder to notice. Also, look here. You were frequenting some of the same places several times in one month. So, if she just has a handful of these. One extra booking, every time you go to one of these places, puts a pretty penny in her pocket each month."

"Right," Gil confirmed.

"Ok," Jack patted Gil on the shoulder, "You know what to do," and he walked back to the dining room to finish the leftovers from the hearty meal Venus had made him the night before.

***

Before Jack could finish his meal, Gil was hollering for him again. "Jack! I got another instruction!"

Jack wiped his mouth, put his napkin down and walked back into the den. "What did she say this time?"

"There were four consecutive calls in a row, spaced 5 minutes apart. The first one said: 'ATM Draw.' The second one said '1,000' The third one said: 'Mailbox Drop" The fourth one said: '6:13 today' "

"6:13? That's an odd time."

"I know. What do you think that means?"

"Well, Beth told you that she makes cash drops by placing an envelope in her own mailbox with the red flag up, right?"

"Yes."

"After 6:00, there are no more mailmen picking up mail."

"That's right."

"But 6:13 is a very specific time."

"Is she trying to test my ability to be precise?"

"Yes. And she has to have someone else there to pick it up only minutes after you're gone. Otherwise, she risks it getting stolen right out of the box."

"So, do I stake it out after my drop?"

"No. The person she assigned to pick it up will be watching you. This time, just drop it off and leave. We'll set someone up next time. If we have time, that is. She only gave you 30 minutes to complete this job."

"Got it," Gil said, as he grabbed for the Lamborghini's keys.

"Oh, and Gil, make sure you build her confidence in you further by using the same ATM machine you've already used to make a withdrawal of this size, on previous occasions. She'll want consistency in a way that makes her believe the account holder won't notice an extra ATM withdrawal. Remember, she mimics the account holder's typical transactions."

"Sure thing! That's the reason I made a lot of big cash withdrawals during the last statement cycle. I knew she wouldn't be able to resist an account like that!"

CHAPTER 17

Venus tossed the fourth burner phone into the pizza oven, and watched it burn. She would finish another glass of champagne before getting dressed for her evening with Jack Smith. Tonight, he would be taking her out for dinner in a fine restaurant in Beverly Hills.

Upon finishing her glass, she stepped out of her secret office and into her walk-in-closet. Tonight was a night for sheer elegance and charm. Now standing on the other side of the Versace dresses, Venus moved through each one to find the perfect dress.

Each of these dresses had been purchased from different stores by her various pawns using their employers' credit or debit cards. The purchase would be made either online or over the phone by a pawn using her regular authority to buy luxury items on behalf of her employer—such as a female employer who was an avid shopper, or a male employer buying a gift for his wife, girlfriend, mistress, or whoever it might be. The best combination was when one of Venus' pawns worked for a couple that included a shopaholic wife and a philandering husband. Neither of whom wanted the other to notice which purchases were made, or when, and both of whom would rely on their personal assistant to do all the expensive shopping for luxury goods, to be picked up in person and discretely delivered to the recipient. These couples were plentiful in Los Angeles; and Venus profited handsomely off of them.

When purchasing on behalf of their employers, the pawns would simply add 1 extra dress to an already expensive purchase, so that the purchase of the stolen dress would not appear alone on the credit card statement, but instead would be mixed in as part of a single transaction, which included the purchase of multiple items at once. It blended in with an already expensive transaction from one department store on a date the pawn's employer would have remembered as an expensive purchase for oneself or a special someone coinciding with a special occassion.

The pawn would always schedule an in-store pickup and receive the items from store employees who knew these pawns by face and name, due to the frequent errands they ran for their bosses, and the frequent purchases their bosses made from the same stores. Before driving back to their employers' home or office, to deliver the authorized purchase item, the pawn would place the extra item from the unauthorized purchase into a box addressed to a suite in a building in Beverly Hills which housed many virtual offices. The suite number belonged to an import/export business which rented virtual office space in a Class A high rise building. Pursuant to Venus' instructions, the pawns would not identify a recipient, but list only the virtual office address. Venus never told any of the purchasing pawns the name of the import/export company. She would instruct them to place a second label on each box, indicating something along the lines of: "For Client Bob A." The pawns were never told what would occur after dropping off the stolen item at this location.

In addition, the operators of the virtual office space believed they were merely handling the legitimate mailing and messenger services required of an import/export company who maintained a presence in the city. The virtual office provider already handled the mail of many other businesses, and therefore, would not be suspicious or even notice who dropped off a package, and who picked it up. In this environment, those dropping off packages could be remote workers or messenger services; and those picking up packages could be clients. Nobody was keeping track.

Once the package was dropped off, Venus would instruct a different pawn to retrieve it. The retrieving pawn was not connected to any of Venus' "clients," but merely served delivery and drop off functions in Venus' network of pawns. This pawn would appear at the building which housed the virtual office, and tell the front desk that he or she was a personal messenger there to pickup a package "For Client Bob A," or whichever client name Venus had instructed the dropping pawn to use on the package's label. Like clockwork, and as part of their ordinary business functions, the virtual office provider would produce the correct package to the retrieving pawn, with no questions asked, and nothing peculiar to remember. With hundreds of businesses utilizing the same location for virtual offices, to send and receive mail, packages and personal deliveries, Venus' system was well hidden. Each of the pawns she used for to retrieve the packages were already employees of legitimate messenger service companies. After receiving a coded call from Venus about the package, they would incorporate these special deliveries into their usual routes and their ordinary business day, just for that little extra cash that would later appear in their mailbox, disguised as junk mail.

The final destination of each package was the same—a warehouse in Dubai. First, Venus would instruct one of her delivery network pawns to pick up the package at the front desk of the virtual office in Los Angeles, then mail it to a virtual office in Dubai. From there, another messenger would pick it up and deliver it to the warehouse. The warehouse was safe from any investigations by authorities, because it was owned by a member of the royal family who stored many of his own unused goods there. He had a sports car fetish, which became a nuisance to his family, who did not want them all piling up at his home. So he bought a warehouse, which served as his personal sports car gallery. He was good friends with Venus, yet clueless of her true identity or her life of crime. He believed he was simply being kind to a good friend, by allowing her to use a portion of his warehouse from which the shipping heiress could conduct her legitimate business of providing the wealthy visitors and shoppers of Dubai with a personalized luxury shopping experience.

This warehouse is where all of Venus' stolen goods ended up. She used the same scheme with her pawns from a similar network structure, she had built in various cities around the western world, including New York, London, Paris, Berlin and Rome. Once the stolen items arrived in the Dubai warehouse, Venus could do what she pleased with them, whether she sold them, or kept some for herself.

Tonight, she would be dressed from head to toe in stolen goods selected for her own personal wardrobe from the warehouse in Dubai. Planning for a night of seduction that would blow Jack's mind, Venus pulled out a black dress, which had lace in all the right places. The dress was in the style of a slip dress, in that it was very thin material with spaghetti strap sleeves. But it was long and form fitting, hugging every inch of her perfect body. The length of it fell to below her knees, with an uneven bottom hem line, shaped like a wave. Her left knee was barely covered, while the right side of the dress came to a point halfway down her shin. It drew one's eyes down to her bright red, but barely there, 4-inch stilettos displaying a beautiful foot wrapped in the thin straps of an open toed shoe. Her toenails were painted bright red, as were her fingernails and lips. The red color of her lips, set against her stark white complexion and black lace dress, made her blue eyes pop with fierce, dazzling beauty. The V-cut top of the dress plunged so low that the skin of her soft, voluptuous breasts promised a man pure pleasure and bliss. She wore her hair up in an elegant but effortless updo to emphasize a sensational display of skin. Diamond earrings cascaded down both sides of her delicate face, ending at her jaw bone.

Now completely dressed for the evening, Venus looked in the mirror and raised her chin, then shook her head slightly, as if in ecstasy. She watched the diamonds dance as they caressed her skin and she imagined Jack's perspective once she had him home tonight, beneath her, while she wore nothing but those diamond earrings. She was going to give him an evening he'd never forget.

***

Jack had reserved them a VIP table in a corner booth where the white, curved, leather bench seat had a back high enough to hide them from view of other diners. A sheer multi-layered curtain, which closed off the booth provided even more privacy. Venus appreciated the intimate setting this offered, but Jack's purpose was discretion. He did not want to accidentally run into any colleagues who might approach the table and blow his cover. He could not tell Venus his true identity, until after his undercover investigation came to a close. She was too immersed in the world into which he offered himself as bait to attract the pawns who would lead him to the suspect. He could not risk telling her his true identity until his work was finished.

Jack and Venus sat very close to each other throughout the dinner. They started with champagne. Having already savored two glasses earlier that evening, the additional glass made Venus feel frisky before the appetizers even arrived. She leaned against Jack, whispered in his ear, and placed her hand on his thigh, caressing it every so gently. Jack kissed her lips, but gently removed her hand. "I'll never make it through dinner, if you keep your hand there," Jack teased. She gave a seductive laugh, tilting her head back, exposing the nape of her neck right down to her plunging neck line. Jack kissed the nape of her neck, then kissed a spot behind her ear. She sighed and trembled at the soft touch of his lips. Then she purred into his ear, "Oh take me home, Jack!" Jack gave her a strong kiss on the lips, forcing his tongue into her mouth and she received it with hunger for more. He suddenly pulled away leaving her almost panting. He stared into her eyes, then she rested her head against his shoulder, knowing he was going to make her wait through the whole dinner. "Soon, my love," she heard him whisper, then she smiled.

As blood flowed to the most sensitive parts of her body, Venus closed her eyes, trying to get ahold of herself. It was going to be even harder for her to make it through dinner. She tried to think of things to distract herself. Numbers, numbers filled her mind. Bank statements, names of "clients," anything to keep her from straddling Jack right where he sat, in this public place, which mocked her with a thin curtain of false privacy.

Before long, Jack and Venus were making small talk, giggling and enjoying the food and drink. Jack held Venus' hand, clasping it firmly and holding it close to him, as if to say, you are mine and I will always protect you. Venus could feel his promising and unrelenting strength, and it made her feel more relaxed than she had ever felt in her life. Pure bliss filled her heart as she looked into Jack's eyes.

When their dinner plates were removed, and the waiter left to place their order for desert, Jack excused himself to go to the restroom. Though it was a common and unremarkable act of stepping away from the table, Venus felt as if something had just been torn from her. The feeling startled her, as she was unaccustomed to feeling so in need of another human being. When the curtain closed behind him, she quickly moved it with one hand, just enough to watch him walk away. For some illogical reason, she had to watch him until he was out of sight. But before he reached the restroom, a woman approached him. Venus narrowed her eyes and watched ever so intently trying to gauge the exchange to determine whether it was a familiar woman or someone who just wanted to stop a handsome stranger. The two were out of earshot, so Venus studied the body language. The woman placed her hands on him, while she spoke to him—a sign of intimacy. While they spoke, she placed her hand on his shoulder, then gradually slid it down his arm and almost grabbed his hand, but Jack moved it away, every so subtly.

The exchange was short, but when it ended, Venus thought she read the woman's lips who said, "Call me, Jack." Jack's back was to Venus so she couldn't see his lips, but she saw him nod. As Jack walked towards the restroom, the woman walked towards Venus but turned while several feet away to meet a group of women at her own table. Before she turned, Venus snapped a picture of her face.

When Jack came back to the table, Venus attempted to gain more information about the woman without sounding jealous or demanding or intrusive. She waited for Jack to get comfortable, then she took a strawberry off his dessert plate and placed it into his mouth. He savored the taste of it, and stole a kiss of her fingers while she still held her hand close to his mouth. She giggled and said, "I missed you while you were gone."

Jack gave a flattered laugh.

"Did you meet anyone interesting out beyond the curtain?" Venus teased.

Jack was honest, "Why yes I did, actually. I ran into an old friend."

"Oh! Tell me more," Venus said, as if intrigued, and she smiled sweetly at Jack.

"Oh, there's not much to tell, she's just an old friend."

"Well, does she have a name?"

"Oh, I'm sorry, darling. Yes she has a name. Her name is Jillian."

Venus nudged him, "Jillian . . ."

"Smart," Jack answered. Her name is "Jillian Smart."

"Ah, that's a nice sounding name. What does she do for a living?"

"She's an attorney for a big law firm in town."

Having heard enough, Venus feigned a deteriorating interest, "I'm sure she's magnificent. With a name like Ms. Smart! But that's enough about her, let's talk about us!" Venus beamed with a bright smile.

"What about us?" Jack said seductively, smiling down at Venus.

"I think you know!" she said, as she tickled him and he laughed.

"I sure do," he said, then he opened the curtain and called out: "Check please!"

CHAPTER 18

When Jack left Venus' bed the next morning, she seemed distracted. She wasn't her usual self. Usually, she would purr sweet nothings into his ear, enticing him for more pleasure. Or she would just snuggle sweetly beside him, and ask him what he wanted her to fix him for breakfast. But this morning was different. Her eyes were searching, as if rapid thought were crossing her mind. She hadn't even come to his side of the bed, but remained on the other half of the California King, with her back to him. He could see her eyes now, only because he'd gotten out of bed and was getting dressed. She wasn't looking at him, but staring off into space, with those searching eyes. She didn't even notice him watching her, as he dressed.

Jack sat on the plush settee against the wall nearest her side of the bed. He leaned forward, resting his elbows on his knees and paused before picking up his sock. He watched her, but she still didn't see him. He wondered what could be troubling her. Not wanting to disrupt her thoughts, he didn't ask her. He tried to read her face, hoping for a clue. He replayed the prior evening in his mind. Still, he could not think of anything that might have troubled her. She certainly gave no sign of it at the restaurant, or afterward, when she gave him another spectacular night in the bedroom. This morning, it was as if someone flipped a switch, and his loving, seductive, beauty was now someone else.

"Venus," he whispered. And she looked up at him. Now, suddenly, her face beamed with a bright smile and her blue eyes shined, "Jack, darling!" she said with glee-filled enthusiasm.

Jack smiled back at her.

"You're already completely dressed!" she noted with surprise, as if she had just seen him for the first time.

"Yes," Jack chuckled.

Venus then lifted the covers, exposing a magnificent goddess-like figure, still nude from the evening before. Jack stared at her body, forgetting entirely the unusual demeanor that had left him wondering, only seconds ago.

Venus walked towards Jack, and his arms instinctively reached for her. She pressed her body against his, as she landed a deep, sensuous kiss on his lips. She felt his body's immediate response between his legs, and she quickly unzipped his pants, springing him free. Then, she lifted her hips, and slipped herself on top of him, as he sighed in ecstasy. She sat hard, and paused as she stared into his eyes. His eyes glazed over in passion and she rode him, slowly, forcefully, purposefully, as her hands gripped his hair tight and she pressed her forehead against his. Her breath began to match his. It was the same rhythm of her movement, as she rode and rode, until together they both let out a cry in unison, as each of their bodies released sweet ecstasy in the same precious moment of completely satisfied bliss.

Now panting, Jack wrapped his strong arms around her, holding her as close to him as possible. With his cheek pressed hard against hers, he whispered in her ear, still breathless, "I love you, Venus."

Venus smiled. Her eyes gleamed with victory, as her mind returned to the rapid thoughts that began her morning. She still planned to learn more about that woman he had spoken to in the restaurant last night.

CHAPTER 19

Gil had one dimple on his left cheek, which showed most prominently when he gave a side smile. He used that side smile today on the same lady at the impound lot from which he obtained the Lamborghini, which was still parked in Jack's Bel Air drive way. His sunglasses shaded his eyes from the bright California sun, but the woman remembered them clearly. She could still imagine the soft, playful brown eyes he had turned on her before. They were the perfect compliment to that cute dimple prominently emphasized by his side smile.

"I need an old junker today," Gil said, now widening his grin, flashing bright white teeth.

"For what?" she tried to argue.

"Just give me one from the forfeiture lot. It won't be missed."

"There aren't too many old junkers. Those aren't the types of cars people usually steal."

Gil roared with laughter. "No. One from the forfeiture lot. You won't be giving these back to their rightful owners. You have some old junkers that were used to commit a crime, don't you? You know, the ones that have already been forfeited after trial."

"I don't know," she said, as she turned to her computer.

"Just let me look around," Gil suggested.

Soon, Gil was weaving his way through a crowded lot of parked cars—some cars still marked with bullet wholes, others too conspicuous for his purpose. Then, finally, he came across the perfect car. It was something that would be driven by the complete opposite of the person he currently played in his role as the Lamborghini-driving assistant of a billionaire. It was a beat up old pick up truck, with license plates from out of state. If parked on the side of a West Hollywood street, it would instantly be assumed to be the car of a tourist who had driven to California. It also created an opportunity for an even better disguise than Gil had originally pictured. With this vehicle, he could use an over-sized cowboy hat to cover the entire crown of his head, down to his eyebrows, thereby disguising his hair color, entirely. The sun glasses, flannel shirt and fake goatee that he could easily slip on while inside the vehicle would add further cover.

This time, Gil was determined to catch and follow the person making the cash pickup from his mailbox. When Beth had first asked for Gil's information to induct him into Charlotte's Angels, he had selected an address in the Hollywood area near Beth's apartment complex. The mailbox there didn't have a red flag to raise, so instead, he would place a red sticker on it, and leave the mailbox unlocked when making cash drops, pursuant to Charlotte's orders. Gil anticipated that another order for a cash drop would come any day now; and he wanted to be ready. He had already surveyed the area near the mailbox. There were multiple spots for street parking around the corner and out of sight from the mailbox. He would park this pickup truck there and move it daily, keeping it only steps away, but still out of sight, and at the ready for when the time came.

CHAPTER 20

Jack was at the country club mingling with friends. He left Venus' home hours ago, but she was still home. To avoid accompanying him to the county club, Venus gave Jack a false excuse about shopping. Now, Venus was safely behind the back wall of her walk in closet, where her work could begin.

Consistent with her usual custom, Venus put business before pleasure, and money before love. That is why she called the Golden Bartender before she called the private investigator.

He was L.A.'s favorite bartender, and he had held that position for 20 years. One might say that the Golden Bartender was the most popular man in L.A.'s night life. He was quick with a patron's favorite drink, and smart with advice he gave, whenever one of them told him secrets they'd never tell their friends. Alcohol lulled his customers into this sense of security, but his charm lulled them even further. He had information. It was valuable information. He could tell you who was cheating on who, among celebrity couples, or who screwed who in any major business deal in Hollywood and beyond. He kept this information secret and reserved it only for his best customers. But that's not why Venus called him today. She called him because of the services he shared with all of his customers. The Golden Bartender set up the wealthiest who's who of every social circle in L.A., at whatever club, lounge or bar they wanted to drink at, on any given night of the week. He had connections at all the hottest places in the city. One phone call was all it took.

The Golden Bartender was everyone's friend. He had that perfect Southern California tan, dirty blonde hair, friendly brown eyes, and a smile that said "welcome home," every time a patron sat at the bar he was tending. Although he was forty-one, he had the physique and energy of a 20 year old. It was probably because of all the surfing he did during the day, before the bar scene became lively and lucrative at night.

One thing all his patrons never knew, was that behind that smile and fun-loving spirit that kept them entertained and happy during their nights out, was a very sharp mind. The only reason he wasn't wheeling and dealing massive amounts of other people's money as a licensed stock broker was because of that minor petty theft conviction, from a long time ago, that he would've been required to disclose in licensing applications. So, he never applied. The Golden Bartender could memorize series of numbers as if he had a photographic memory. He could calculate math in his head like a calculator; and he could observe, remember and analyze patterns even faster than a computer. None of his patrons knew this about him, except one mysterious woman who had observed him silently from the far end of the bar approximately 15 years ago. Venus' secret weapon in life was the ability to instantly determine a person's weaknesses, strengths and special abilities. From that distant seat at the bar, she had watched the beautiful young man satisfy every customer in an overcrowded bar without missing a beat. She noticed him tap in credit card numbers for customers who'd forgotten their wallets. "Don't worry. I got you," she heard him say, and observed that his customers never asked him how. She could see that he was not pulling up a card on file; rather, he was tapping in a number from memory. So, when this gorgeous, young surfer-looking bartender gave his phone number to a patron who asked him to "hook him up" for the next weekend at the newest and most-happening club, Venus wrote down the Golden Bartender's phone number on a cocktail napkin and slipped it into her purse. He never saw her. And he still doesn't know who the mysterious woman is who calls him every now and then with a new account.

Approximately three weeks after she had first observed the Golden Bartender, Venus began testing him. He failed five times in a row, reacting as if some lunatic were calling. Venus did not give up because the talent and ability he possessed was a very rare find. She justified deviating from her three-attempt rule because no other pawn had made the initial introduction. Therefore, it was natural, she thought, for him to wonder what stalker was calling him with such strange coded statements. Finally, she used his talents to her advantage. She began a pattern until he deciphered her code. His first task was easy: "Leave the lime on the bar." The same evening, Venus instructed various pawns to go out to the bar where he was employed, and place a ten dollar bill under every wedge of lime they saw on the bar, throughout the entire evening. The Golden Bartender caught on very quickly. He began leaving a wedge of lime next to every drink he poured for the next three weeks.

Venus' next instruction was delivered through a series of phone calls, each one spread out, 5 minutes apart:

"Refund."

"Every other one."

"Young Prince."

"Wait 40 days."

The Golden Bartender knew exactly who she was referring to and what she was asking him to do. 30 days later, Venus saw the evidence of his compliance in the bank statement of one of her royal “clients” who drank daily, where the Golden Bartender worked, during the prince’s annual 3-month trip to L.A. The prince's assistant was a pawn of Venus. She had instructed the pawn to collect all receipts for that month and fax them to Venus, with the bank statements. Venus saw that the Golden Bartender had refunded an amount equal to one half of all the drinks the prince ordered over the course of the month. This brought the Golden Bartender into Venus' network. He had passed the qualifying test.

Before she advanced him to that next level, Venus rewarded him. She instructed 10 different pawns to deliver $1,000 cash, each, in a sealed envelope placed under their drink for the bartender to pick up, like a tip. This occurred on the 40th day after her last phone call to the Golden Bartender. In addition to the cash, the pawns were also ordered to slip a note into each of their envelopes, with the words "thank you for the Rs," to ensure the Golden Bartender knew he had been compensated for a mission accomplished.

Next, Venus set up an account that looked very much like the prince's expense account, with a similar name, at a different bank, in another jurisdiction. It was that account number she used in her next instruction to the Golden Bartender, through a 4-call series. In her first call she said, “Deposit.” Five minutes later, her second call said, “Prince.” Five minutes later her third call said, “Refund.” Five minutes later, in her fourth and final call, she quickly rattled off the numbers of the new bank account.

Thereafter, Venus was pleasantly surprised to notice, that the Golden Bartender was a self-starter. After he received the account number into which refunds would be misdirected, he began making additional refunds, each month, without being asked. The bar he worked was inside a luxury hotel in Beverly Hills, which frequently rewarded its high profile clients with various perks and credits. The Golden Bartender took advantage of this system, and refunded, into the new account, transactions consistent with the patterns of credits the hotel was already in the habit of giving to the prince. Noticing his self-initiation, Venus quickly realized that adding new targets to the bartender’s list, would be very easy. All she had to do was identify her target, and the account into which refunds should be sent; then, the Golden Bartender would calculate patterns and refunds that could go undetected for an indefinite period of time. He was her most valuable and dependable pawn.

From the bartender’s perspective, it was the perfect crime. He could never be accused of taking the funds himself, because they went into an account he never touched or had anything to do with. Thus, he encouraged his unknown benefactor through his good work, and he trusted the mysterious female to notice, and to compensate him, in good time. He was also very quick to form more stability, early in this budding relationship, by communicating with her, his preferred method of compensation. Receiving large tips at the bar he worked was too risky. In order to further cover his tracks, he slipped in his own coded message the next time Venus called with a new target. As quickly as he could, before she hung up, he said: "No more tips," knowing that she would make two to three more calls over the next 15 minutes. In her second call, he said: "PO Box 9812." In her third call, he said, "Santa Monica." Venus smiled at the brilliance of the Golden Bartender, and knew this would be a long and lucrative relationship.

Now, 15 years later, the Golden Bartender was netting Venus $500,000 per year in regular steady income. Today, Venus instructed him to supplement that income. She made a series of calls to the Golden Bartender, wherein she gave the following instructions:

"JAK LLC"

"Refund 1"

"Every Round"

"New Mexico"

She ended that series of calls with one final call where she rattled off several numbers. The numbers constituted the routing and bank account number of an account held by JAK LLC—a company with the exact same name as the account holder on the bank statements Gil had previously faxed to Venus. However, it was a different company entirely, because it had been formed in New Mexico, not California, where Jack and Gil had formed the limited liability company, which held the expense account for their undercover operation.

Having completed her instructions to her most lucrative pawn, Venus, placed her perfectly foamed cappuccino on her desk, and walked over to her white marble end table where the other burner phone lie waiting. She picked it up, and sat down on her chaise lounge, swinging her feet up, as she leaned back against the arm, and faced her waterfall. Then, she dialed a phone number she knew by heart.

She called a legitimate private investigation company whom she regularly used under the guise of an international law firm researching the assets of individuals against whom her law firm was in litigation. Her false law firm had a danish name, and the burner phone she used had a danish phone number. The investigator was polite and attentive, because this Danish law firm had been an excellent source of income over the years. Despite researching individuals for a living, he never bothered to research his own clients. It didn't bother him in the least, that this client always paid its bills in cash, and never gave an address to which an invoice could be sent, but would merely check in occasionally to receive an oral statement of amounts due, while collecting an oral report from the investigator about the subject of the investigation.

Today, Venus' purpose was disguised, but her instructions were clear, despite the thick Danish accent with which she spoke:

"Her name is Jillian Smart," said Venus, "She works at a large law firm in Los Angeles, California, though we do not know the name of that law firm. Our own preliminary investigation leads us to believe that she may be hiding assets with a friend of hers—a Bel Air billionaire from Texas. His name is Jack Smith. That is all I know about the subject. Please investigate every connection you can find between the subject and the billionaire. Your job is to investigate their romantic history, so that we may determine whether to investigate his assets as well. For now, please focus only on the relationship between the two. This is an important case for our law firm. We expect to obtain a large judgment against the subject. Please assign someone to follow her, listen to her conversations, and report back about all information you discover that links her to Jack Smith. Please start immediately. She was seen with him, at a restaurant last night."

The investigator took scant notes, which he would destroy after completing his investigation. He wrote down two names and a few words: Jillian Smart. L.A. Law firm; Jack Smith. Texas Billionaire.

CHAPTER 21

Jack's work had never allowed him to spend this much time with one woman. For the first time in his distinguished career, this novel, undercover role allowed him to work while also developing a healthy relationship with a woman. This was unlike his prior relationship with Jillian and other accomplished women, where Jack and his mate would sometimes get so lost in their own career demands, that neither of them really noticed how quickly weeks or months passed by without ever seeing each other—especially when Jack was in trial. The career women new it came with the territory, and had the same bad habits themselves. The young women seeking a benefactor were irritable and impatient and would let their insecurities get the better of them, ultimately resulting in the deterioration of the relationship.

In contrast, Jack's relationship with Venus was developing with the smooth and natural beauty of an old fashioned love. They had time. And in that time, he got to know her soul. He knew what made her laugh. He knew what made her soft. He knew what ignited her passion, whether it be politics, art, or lovemaking. He allowed her to dote on him, and she seemed to love every minute of doing so. She was the solution to everything that had been wrong with previous serious girlfriends. Though powerful and dominant with her femininity, she always let Jack be the man. He felt chivalrous, strong and manly whenever he was with her.

The most exciting thing about Venus was how well she could be two women at once. In the daytime, and while others were around, she was the perfectly mannered, girl next door who could bake and cook and be the dream housewife of the 1950's. But when night fell, she transformed into the Vixen of his bedroom, taunting him, teasing him, and pleasuring him until she blew his mind. And on some nights, she would be the sweet love of his life, letting him take control, and give her sweet, caring love. She was everything a man could ever dream of.

Today, on this sunny, Sunday afternoon, Jack lie comfortably against the plush cushion of his pool lounger, as he watched Venus at the opposite end of the pool, in her one piece swimsuit, bathing under the waterfall that spilled into his pool. It was a sight to behold. The backdrop of fresh greenery and bright flowers surrounded her, as the plants curved around that end of the pool, above, behind and around the waterfall, sprawling along the sides of the pool, inching towards the edge of the water, as if it were a scene from heaven. Beneath the waterfall, a goddess bathed. His goddess, Venus.

She wet her hair and moved her head from side to side, letting the water fall all about her. She faced him, but did not look in his direction. Her eyes were closed as if the water caressing her skin aroused her. Soon, her right hand lightly touched her left shoulder, and one finger crept beneath the strap. As if caressing herself, her right hand moved down her shoulder and across her breast, which sprang free from the swimsuit by the swift movement of her hand. She raised her chin high, allowing the water to cascade down her bare breast. Jack's body responded in an instant. His eyes widened as he leaned forward and his manhood grew. With only one breast exposed, Venus caressed her own skin, moving her right hand across her covered breast, then up towards her right shoulder, and down came the strap on that side. Soon she was completely nude and her body gleamed beneath the water. Jack sprang out of his seat and dove into the pool, swimming swiftly under water towards her. He burst out of the water with a splash, inches from her nude body.

"Oh Jack!"she squealed as she wrapped her arms around him. He lifted her up by her buttocks with both hands, and she wrapped both legs tight around him—the waterfall cascading down their faces and their chests. Jack slipped himself inside her and she sighed sharply and moaned delicately, as he rocked her, and rocked her, and rocked her, until they both came together in ecstasy.

Exhausted from pleasure, his strong arms lifted her out of the pool and laid her gently on the concrete warmed by the sun. Placing two hands near her naked and wet body, on the warm concrete, he lifted himself up out of the pool with two muscular arms, water pouring all over her body as it dripped from his. First he lied on top of her to give her a gentle kiss, then he rolled to the side, lying beside her, and cradled her in his arms, as they both lie panting heavily. When he caught his breath, he kissed her neck, then her cheek, then her lips. In a state of pure bliss, she lie flat on the ground, arms and legs putty, as she indulged in every moment. When he put his lips to her ears, he whispered, "Venus, be my wife." Her wide smile and euphoric sigh was all the response he needed. He placed his left hand at the nape of her neck, then slowly drew it down her skin, with a touch so light it felt like the wind, until he reached that spot between her legs; and with one finger, he slowly brought her to orgasm again, but he took his time, as he watched her move and writhe in uncontrollable passion and pleasure.

CHAPTER 22

Gil arrived five minutes early. He leaned against the Lamborghini and stared at his wrist watch until it turned to exactly 6:17 p.m. Then he placed an envelope containing $1,000 cash into the mailbox, and shut the box without letting it latch. He placed a red circle sticker on the outside, then jogged around the corner.

Once inside the dumpy old pickup truck that he had parked there earlier, he changed his shirt, placed a false goatee onto his handsome face, added sunglasses and an oversized cowboy hat, then sprinted back to the corner from where he could watch the mailbox.

At exactly 6:19 p.m., a man rounded the opposite corner. He walked a dog on a leash. When the man and the dog reached the mailbox, Gil barely heard the man's voice, carried on the warm breeze, which tickled Gil's false goatee against his face. Were it not for this breeze, Gil would not have heard it. The man whispered one word: "Now." As if on command, the dog stopped, began sniffing towards the mailbox, then sat down in front of it. The man picked up the dog with both hands, and loudly stated, "Let's go, Rover," while holding the dog directly in front of Gil's mailbox, completely blocking it from view.

Gil watched closely because there was something else peculiar about the man. He wore gloves on a hot day. With his sharp 20/20 vision, Gil saw the man place one hand into his pocket, while using the other hand to hold the dog in position, blocking the mailbox. The movement was so swift that Gil did not see the man reach into the mailbox. All he saw was the man's free hand move towards the pocket of his windbreaker. Because both the gloves and the windbreaker were black, the white corner of the envelope peaking above the man's thumb, was visible from a distance.

When the man put the dog down, Gil ducked around the corner and waited. As soon as he passed Gil's corner, Gil followed. Two blocks down the street, the man entered a blue sedan, and sat in the driver's seat. Gil photographed the license plate quickly, ready to sprint back to the pickup and follow. However, Gil noticed that the man had not started the vehicle, but instead began reaching into the passenger seat as if arranging items, apparently placed there from before. So, Gil approached the vehicle, slowly. As he neared the vehicle, he could see the man separating the $100 bills, two at a time. Then, he stuffed two bills at a time into separate envelopes. Gil rushed to the man's vehicle to get a closer look through the open passenger window. Gil startled the man, as he blurted out, a thick Southern accent while shoving his head inside the man's car window: "Howdy, could ya help a cowboy out?"

The man jumped in his seat, nearly dropping what he held in his hands, and jerked his head towards the window, practically shouting, "What!"

"Ya see, sir. I'm lost. Could ya give me directions," Gil said as he peered around the vehicle from behind his dark sunglasses.

"Uh, sure, I guess, so," said the man, as he scrunched the last two $100 bills in his hand, and slipped them into his pocket.

Ignoring the man's instructions given in response to Gil's false request, Gil focused his eyes on four envelopes lying face up on the passenger seat. They had already been stamped and addressed beforehand. The man had already sealed them. No return address appeared on any of the envelopes. Gil immediately recognized the names of two recipients appearing on the preprinted envelopes. Gil's own alias was typed on one, and addressed to the same mailbox into which he had just placed the $1,000. Beth's name and address appeared on another. The other two envelopes bore recipient names that were also vaguely familiar. Gil also noticed that the envelopes were self adhesive. The strips that once covered the self adhesive line were now littered on the floorboard. Gil assumed the stamps were also self-adhesive, losing all hope of collecting a DNA sample upon receipt of his own envelope. As Gil's mind inventoried the scene, the two familiar names suddenly rang a bell. Each name was on the list of pawns already identified in the investigation, from documents delivered to them by Detective Jones.

***

As Jack stood in his master bedroom tying his tie for another elegant evening with Venus, he could hear Gil slam the door, as he entered the Bel Air mansion, cussing loudly. Jack hurried down the stairs to find out what was wrong.

Seeing Jack mid-way down the stairs, Gil exclaimed: "She just won't leave us a trail! Are we ever going to find this woman? She just won't leave a trial!" He cursed angrily, and continued, "I'd rather be chasing drug dealers!"

"Hold on, Gil, calm down a minute. Tell me what happened."

Gil explained to Jack what he had observed, and Jack said only two words: "That's incredible."

Gil carried on, still angry, throwing his hands up and almost hollering, "I thought I could follow this guy to a bank where he would make a deposit, then we could subpoena the bank."

"What bank did you think was still open after 6:30?"

"I don't know!" shouted Gil in frustration, "I wanted to follow him somewhere, to learn something! But she's too smart. She's recycling the same cash that's stolen by ATM withdrawals from her victim's accounts to pay her pawns in cash."

"What do you mean?" asked Jack.

After Gil explained what he had observed, Jack elaborated, "So, she's got the pawns wrapped into a Ponzi scheme with their own stolen money."

"Yeah!" shouted Gil, "She says give me $1,000 then she gives them back $200!"

"Amazing," said Jack, "So that's how she runs her payroll. We'll never find a single banking transaction that will connect her to any of these pawns."

"No! We wont!" exclaimed Gil, still frustrated, "Even the guy picking up the cash paid himself with a portion of the money. $200 each. I guess she believes in equal pay! Good for her!" Gil veered off into sarcasm to ease his frustration.

Jack sat down, put his elbow on the table, and rested his cheek on his fist. He sat thinking while Gil remained stewing. Then a ray of light came to his mind, which brightened his face with a smile. "Not all is lost, Gil. You now know what this man looks like. You ran his license plate and now have his identity. When it comes time to take down these pawns, we'll arrest him and he'll have the names and addresses of many more pawns on her payroll." Jack then pulled out the thick stack of documents that Detective Jones had previously delivered, and said, "the larger we grow this list of pawns to arrest, the more of a chance we'll have to find a link to their leader."

Gil perked up in response to the piles of evidence already gathered, "That's right," he agreed with Jack, "every criminal makes one small mistake at some point or another. The more pawns we identify, the more likely we'll find where she slipped and left a paper trail from one of them to her."

"Speaking of paper trails," said Jack, "what have you seen so far by way of refunds made against our dummy account that you've been lavishly spending from?"

"Nothing, so far. The refunds don't return to the same account. Remember? We have to figure out how they are re-directed to a different account."

"Didn't Beth say she was required to shred refund confirmation emails?"

"Yes, but so far I haven't received any."

"So, we wait, then," said Jack, as he stood to walk back up the stairs to finish dressing for an elegant and romantic evening with Venus.

CHAPTER 23

Jillian Smart was finally relaxing after a long day at the office. It was late in the evening, and she sat at her favorite table, in her favorite restaurant, across from her favorite person—her law partner Pete Farwel. Pete wore the same colored pink shirt that he had worn at the party where he first met Jack. It was the party where Jillian paraded Jack before her colleagues, like a prize-winning horse. Pete Farwel loved to tease Jillian about the gorgeous men she had dated over the years that he'd known her, and he usually did so with his infamously bombastic personality. Pete was adamant that Jack Wayne was the best treat Jillian had ever brought to a party, and Pete was going to make her dish everything she knew about him, now.

Unfortunately, the man seated at the table next to them was listening to every word.

Oblivious to the man seated there, Jillian and her colleague indulged in their usual custom of drowning out a long, arduous business day with their favorite beverages. They dined in an elegant restaurant at the top of a building high enough to give them a spectacular view of the city. Jillian drank a vodka martini, flavored with something pink, and adorned with a red rose lying atop the glass, balanced by its shortened stem; and Pete drank a dry gyn martini with two pepper-stuffed olives soaking in the gyn, held steady by a silver toothpick. Jillian sipped her drink, and Pete guzzled his. Pete always became louder and more bombastic when he drank. This made it easy for the man seated at the table next to them to capture every fine detail.

"Oh come on, Jillian! You never dish," Pete complained. "It's time you learned to kiss and tell!"

Jillian shook her head profusely.

"Oh come on!" nudged Pete. "There's no harm in me living vicariously through you. That man is straight as a board, I could NEVER convince him to swing MY way!" Pete bellowed with laughter and Jillian joined him in a giggle.

"Oh stop, Pete! That's so inappropriate!"

"What?" Pete emphasized the word as if falsely accused. Then he looked around the room gesturing with both arms and announced: "He's not here! And I won't tell, and you won't tell, and HE won't tell!" Pete pointed at the man seated at the table next to them, who jumped with a start at the sudden attention he had just received.

"Well?" Pete demanded, "YOU won't tell him, will you?" he teased the stranger, who looked around nervously. Then Pete bellowed with laughter and waived a dismissive hand, "I'm just kidding! Relax."

Jillian laughed softly and excused her friend's behavior. She politely asked the stranger's forgiveness, and promised not to disrupt his dinner again.

"That's ok, ma'am," the stranger replied before Pete bellowed an interruption:

"Oh! He doesn't mind, Jillian! We're better company than that napkin ring on his table!"

The man looked down, embarrassed, and Jillian apologized to him again.

"Well," insisted Pete, "he's having dinner alone. We should ask him to join us, shouldn't we, Jillian?"

This time the man spoke. "Thank you sir, that is very kind of you, but I'm dining alone tonight because I'm actually having a working dinner." The man tapped the laptop on the chair beside him, and said, "As soon as I finish my meal, I will pull out my laptop and continue my work."

"Well, you're no fun," Pete said dismissively as he waved his hand at the man and turned his head back to Jillian.

The man chuckled, relieved that Jillian's companion finally forgot his presence. The man then re-started the voice recording app on his smart phone that lie next to his dinner plate, and he proceeded to eat and drink with both hands as if completely oblivious to the conversation taking place beside him. However, the man was paying close attention to every word.

Pete continued bombarding Jillian with questions about Jack Wayne. It was the wrong Jack—not the one the man was listening for; but the surname "Smith" was so generic, that he chose to keep his attention keen, in case it turned out to be the same Jack that he was instructed to investigate regarding a relationship with Jillian Smart.

"Ok," Pete continued, "So at the party, you said, he was not just any ordinary Deputy D.A., but that he was on his way to becoming THE D.A. Is that true?"

Jillian beamed with pride and a wide smile, "Yes."

"Jillian! This could be THE one! I mean, he's not just drop dead gorgeous, he's smart! And sophisticated! And distinguished! And he puts to shame all the trial lawyers in our firm!" Pete bellowed again with roaring laughter.

Because Pete was a transactions lawyer, he didn't feel threatened by Jack's trial skills; but instead, respected that about him. That was why Pete was immensely entertained by Jillian's parade of Jack Wayne at his party, where she made all the other civil litigators, with whom Jillian competes, feel less like trial lawyers in Jack's presence. Pete persisted, "Jillian! You'd have the trophy spouse of all trophy spouses!"

Pete's enthusiasm suddenly waned when he noticed that Jillian looked down with sadness.

"What?" Pete asked, as he reached across the table to rub Jillian's arm. "Why so sad? You're both busy trial lawyers. It's normal for you to be out of touch for several weeks. I mean, you've been in trial. He's probably been in trial. Didn't you say that your relationship sometimes has weeks-long breaks that neither one of you notice, because you're both so busy?"

"Yes. But this has been a months-long break."

"Well, you've been in that monstrous trial for months now, I'm sure he'll understand. You should give him a call."

Jillian looked away, her eyes hesitant and her face despondent.

"You have to call him, Jillian. I mean, you've let some good ones get away because of the demands of your career, but THIS one, you don't let go. Call him, Jillian."

"I can't."

"Why not?"

"I saw him with someone else."

Pete gasped. "Who!?" he demanded.

"I don't know who she is."

"Where'd you see them?"

"Here."

"When?"

"Two weeks ago."

"Well, are you sure they were dating?"

"Yes. They were behind that curtain at that VIP table, there." Jillian pointed, and as she did, the man seated at the table next to them discretely followed her finger with his eyes.

"Did you talk to him?"

"Yes, he bumped into me when he got up to walk to the restroom."

"Well, what was the conversation like?"

"He wasn't the same."

"How do you mean?"

"The spark was gone. He used to have a spark when he spoke to me, but this time, it felt like a stranger being polite."

"Well, what did the she-devil that was with him look like? There aren't too many who can compete for a man's attention against you," Pete insisted.

"Oh, this one could," Jillian said with absolute certainty.

"Well, what was the slut wearing?" Pete asked.

Jillian looked up with a sigh, as slight disdain filled her laugh. "She did kind of look like a slut," Jillian agreed.

"Well describe the witch to me. I need to picture who could have that affect on him."

As Jillian described Venus' look from head to toe, from her hair style, to her eye color to the earrings, dress and shoes she wore, the man at the table seated next to them took copious notes on the napkin on the opposite side of his dinner plate. He listed the date, time, restaurant, and VIP table identifying the moment Jillian Smart had bumped into Jack Wayne. He also listed every detail Jillian described of the woman who accompanied him.

CHAPTER 24

When she didn't answer, Jack Wayne turned the knob and found that it was unlocked. So, he let himself into her house. She had said, "don't be late," so he wanted to make sure he arrived on time. When he walked in, he did not see her, but he could hear Venus' feminine voice arguing.

"You sold me a lemon! I ought to sue you. I'll sue you for fraud! Black smoke was emanating from the tail pipe! How could that be? It's a brand new car!"

Five seconds of silence passed, then she raised her voice again: "I told you! I dropped it off at your lot with a note in the window the same night I bought it."

Another pause.

"Well, how should I know!?" she exclaimed. "It's your responsibility after I put it on your lot."

She paused again.

"No! I parked it in the back, behind the building. Yes, on the street. Well, fine, technically it's not on your lot, but it's as close as I could put it after hours, with your lot all locked up."

Jack smiled at her naivety, while he listened to her half of the conversation. He shook his head, still smiling while wondering why she would do such a silly thing, and not just wait until they opened the next day so she could hand the keys to a person. His thoughts were interrupted when he heard her again:

"How should I know where your surveillance cameras are. It's not my fault you don't have one pointed in that direction. If the car is missing, that's your problem not mine. I gave it back to you weeks ago, actually months ago."

Jack's eyebrows arched, and he almost started up the stairs to help her solve her problem, but then he remembered that he had to keep his identity a secret, and he couldn't offer to help her with the missing car. He sat down on her couch waiting for her to end the call and come downstairs. Venus continued:

"Of course I reversed the wire! That black smoke billowed out of that vehicle only two blocks down the road! No. . . uh, ... no sir, the wire transfer was not cancelled before it went through. It was reversed. You can call my banker and ask for the file. I guarantee you the wire was confirmed, then I reversed it after I saw that black smoke billowing out of the car. I saw the confirmation of the wire transfer while I was sitting in your dealership, and so did your salesperson!"

Jack became more interested, wanting to use his lawyerly skills to take over the call and protect her from a car dealership that might be taking advantage of her. He resisted. He forced himself to sit still and not blow his cover.

"I don't care what the email says! That must be a mistake! I saw the confirmation with my own eyes."

She paused, then gasped,

"I should call the police on you! You're the fraud! I don't have the car, so why should you get my money! . . . If you dare! I'll sick so many lawyers on you, your dealership will be closed in a heartbeat!"

. . .

"No, you calm down."

. . .

"Yes. It was blue. It was the blue Bugatti."

Jack's eyes popped in wonder. He stood and looked out her window. He was not mistaken. A brand new blue Bugatti, with no license plate, was sitting in her driveway. It was the same one he'd seen her drive before.

The crime-solver in Jack began to stir, but he knew there had to be a reasonable explanation. Perhaps she bought one from a different dealership. The other day he had seen dealer plates on the car. Today, he saw only a temporary license sticker in its window that hadn't been there before. It was odd that such a rare car could be replaced so easily. Shoving these thoughts from his mind, Jack quelled the Senior Deputy District Attorney inside him and resumed his charming billionaire demeanor. He had to do so quickly, because she was coming down the stairs now; but he couldn't pull himself away from the window. Jack continued staring at the shiny, blue sports car in her driveway. He scanned every inch of the vehicle with keen eyes, looking for any other marking that could confirm it was a different car than the one she had been arguing about over the telephone.

"Jack!" she exclaimed with a surprise, "I didn't hear you come in."

Jack whirled around, "Sorry, dear. You said don't be late."

"Well, how long have you been standing there?"

"Long enough to know you need a lawyer."

"But, but, . . . I . . . "

"Don't worry. The lemon law lawyers sometimes work on a contingency. How much money did that slimy salesman get out of you?"

"Oh." She sighed with relief. "Oh, never mind that. I have a long list of lawyers on speed dial. Besides, I had him back tracking by the time I hung up. I think I'll wait for him to make his next move before I start running up my own legal bills. I think I convinced him to just let his insurance company take care of it. He huffed and puffed, but he finally agreed with me, that the car must've been stolen off the street. Also, when he threatened to sue me for quote: 'being stupid enough to leave the car there,' I told him I'd counter sue for fraud, for selling me that lemon."

"I see," Jack nodded.

It was not lost on Venus that Jack had been looking out the window when she had come down the stairs, so she quickly added an important lie: "Also, I have a new one now! See, it's in my driveway! I bought it from a different dealership."

"You must really like blue," Jack noted.

"Yes," Venus breathed, as she batted her eyelashes, and curved her lips slowly into a seductive smile, "it matches my eyes."

She gazed into his eyes, while completing her slow decent down the last few steps, with such feminine power, that she lured him from the window. The seductive, Venus, knew how to distract Jack with the slightest movement of her body, triggering his male instincts to breed not think. He involuntarily walked towards her, each of his steps in synch with her pace. Jack smiled as he met her at the bottom of the staircase. She wrapped her arms around his neck and pressed her soft breasts into his chest, tilting her chin up, offering him her lips. He placed a strong, possessive kiss over her lips. She combed her fingers through his hair, pressing her breasts deeper into his chest, as she released an encouraging moan. Jack's powerful, possessive kiss persisted, as his hands moved up her body.

A few moments later they were in her master bedroom and all had been forgotten—the phone call, the car in the drive, and the reason she'd invited him over in the first place. While the dinner she had prepared was burning in the oven, the two of them burned even hotter in the bedroom.

CHAPTER 25

Today was the hardest Gil had worked during the entire undercover operation. He spent hours scanning hundreds of pages of documents produced in response to subpoenas that were issued to trace the refund activity on the bank account used to bait Charlotte. Now, instead of a billionaire's assistant, he had to play the role of forensic accountant. Although, at some point the state would hire a real forensic accountant, Gil was eager to look for anything that could help them plan their next move towards identifying and capturing Charlotte.

Gil had already discovered that the first brilliant thing Charlotte did was to form limited liability companies, in different states, which had the same name as JAK LLC. That way, Charlotte could open a bank account with the same name, which made it easy for the pawns at the various businesses to refund transactions into those accounts. Doing so would avoid detection of their wrongdoing. With the same customer name, supervisors who saw the refunds, would believe the refund or credit went back to the same customer.

Having discovered this, Gil arranged to have all corporate records and bank records of these copycat LLCs to be subpoenaed. Today, he was reviewing those voluminous documents.

The first folder he picked up contained corporate formation documents. He carefully reviewed every page. As he did so, he learned that Charlotte formed these LLCs only in states that did not require disclosure of the owner of the LLC. There was not a single individual identified as the owner of any of them. Instead, only the organizer was listed. The organizer was an online company that opened thousands of LLCs per year, on behalf of others. That service company was the only name that appeared in any accessible records for the LLCs Charlotte created to copycat JAK LLC.

Frustrated by this situation, Gil then picked up another folder that Detective Jones had dropped off recently. It contained documents obtained from subpoenas issued to that online company. Gil flipped through page after page after page. What he found was astonishing, frustrating, and impressive all at once. Gil was astonished by the meticulous discipline of the person he was investigating. He was frustrated by the dead end he encountered. He was impressed, yet again, by the brilliance of the thief he tried to chase, only to be left feeling like he was chasing his own tail. The documents that he thought would lead him to the thief, only lead him to himself. When he first opened this folder, he felt optimistic by the language of the subpoena, which sought from the subpoenaed party: "all records showing payment from the party that hired you to form JAK LLC." Gil was certain that responses to this subpoena would reveal the identity of the person who ordered the formation of the copycat company, or would at least reveal a money trail that would lead to that person.

Instead, Gil saw that Charlotte had paid the online company that formed the copycat LLCs with an electronic check drawn off of the same bank account that Gil and Jack were using in their investigation.

Gil laughed out loud at the simplicity of her brilliance. It was easy for Charlotte to create a money trail directing anyone who looked for it back to the victim she stole from, because she had access to the routing number and bank account number from the bank statements that Gil had been dutifully sending her, every month.

Much like the Ponzi scheme of paying her pawns from the same cash they stole, it was becoming very clear that Charlotte's criminal operation was entirely funded by stolen money that would never trace back to the master thief.

Gil sighed as he closed the folder and tossed it to one side. However, he remained determined. He was going to catch this thief, somehow.

He now picked up the last folder. It contained the bank records of the copycat LLCs into which the refunds were directed. With only one trail left to follow, Gil read these documents with keen attention to each and every bank statement, transaction receipt and wire confirmation. It was imperative that he determine where the money ended up.

After he completed his review of all these documents, Gil determined that each time, it was the same. Refunds never stayed in the copycat LLC accounts. Daily wire transfers sent the money out of the copycat LLC's bank account and into a small bank in a foreign country, near the Swiss border.

This investigation would soon become international.

CHAPTER 26

The sleeping couple began to stir, while still wrapped in each other's embrace from the splendid evening they shared. As the sunlight glimmered through a peek in Venus' silk drapes, her eyes slowly opened. She hated the thought of getting out of bed, but it was already late in the morning. They had slept in longer than she thought wise. Last night, she had to give Jack an evening of a lifetime, in order to get his mind off that blue Bugatti she found him staring at when she had come down the stairs. The evening also left her exhausted; though still glowing, because it was also a night of a lifetime for her too. As she stirred, Jack's arms gripped her tighter and he moaned, "not yet." She smiled and sank back into the soft, feather bed. Jack began to shift, to position himself on top of her; but, with as much will power as she could muster, she gently pushed him back and whispered delicately, "no." Her heart was pounding and the soft spot between her legs was aching with desire; but, she couldn't let him distract her from her important mission. Today marked a deadline she had previously set, and it must be kept.

Jack looked at Venus with surprise and her heart sank. She hated having to tell him, no. She wrapped her arms around his neck and gave him a soft kiss on the lips. "I wish I could," she murmured, "but I have an appointment." Jack smiled and relaxed, rolling over to lay flat on his back. He put one arm behind his head and looked straight up at the ceiling as he let out a long sigh.

Venus rolled towards him, onto her right shoulder and lifted her left hand to play with the hair on his chest.

"So, what's the appointment for?" Jack asked her.

"I'm going shopping," Venus lied.

"You make appointments for that?"

"I have to get a dress fitted," she continued her deceit.

Jack smiled. "A dress fitted. That sounds promising," he said as his grin widened.

Venus sank deeper into the bed wanting to stay longer. She nuzzled Jack and closed her eyes.

"Describe the dress to me," Jack nudged, "is it white?"

Venus' eyes popped open and she looked into Jack's face, as she smiled brightly at his question.

He looked into her eyes and said, "Make sure to look at rings while you're shopping."

Venus' mouth popped open as she gasped delicately.

Jack continued, "Diamond ones. I want to know what you like."

Venus squealed with delight and practically jumped on top of Jack kissing his face all over.

Jack enjoyed it for a few seconds, then smacked her naked bottom, and said, "Now get dressed. You have some shopping to do."

"Gladly!" Venus exclaimed. Then, she gave him one long kiss before sliding out of bed. Jack watched her go. This was the view he loved best, seeing the morning light shinning on her magnificent nude body. His bliss was short-lived, as she quickly wrapped herself in a plush cotton robe. "Awww," Jack moaned with slight disappointment, as he lifted the covers off of himself and began to dress. Now, unable to contain her excitement,

Venus rushed over to him, still wrapped in her robe, and offered more snuggles and more kisses, as he dressed. She hoped his hands would find his way under her robe; because now, the mission that was on her mind when she first woke, seemed far less important. But his hands remained chaste, and she silently damned him for being such an honorable guy, respecting her wishes, from when she declined him moments ago; but, she also loved him for it. Venus gave him one last tight hug before reluctantly pulling away.

When he was dressed, she accompanied him down the stairs, and he indulged her in one long passionate kiss at the door, before he exited to take the short walk back to the Bel Air mansion he occupied during his under cover operation.

Venus leaned against the door and gazed up at the ceiling, unseeing. Dreams that had never fully formed in her mind before were now vivid. The fluttering in her chest and her stomach were new too. She was elated with pure happiness and joy, with an intensity she'd never known. She looked up the staircase, now less eager to climb them. For she was certain now, that Jillian Smart posed no threat to her relationship with Jack. Therefore, the call to get the results from the investigator could wait. But not for too long, because she had given the investigator a deadline to deliver his initial results, and she would make him keep it, just to keep him on his toes.

***

When Jack entered his own Bel Air mansion, he called out for Gil; and Gil hurried out of the kitchen, still wiping his mouth, after breakfast.

"Any news?" asked Jack.

"Yes!" said Gil, "I think we have a lead!"

"Fantastic. What is it?"

"I have it all laid out in the den, let's go in there."

***

Meanwhile, two doors down, in their Bel Air neighborhood, Venus leaned against the arm of her chaise lounge inside her secret room. She watched the water cascade beautifully down her waterfall and noticed that it was shimmering more than usual. Everything in the room seemed more vivid—the colors, the shine, the softness of the chaise lounge. She curled her knees up to her chest and sipped on her cappuccino. She wasn't quite ready to ruin this new happiness with a phone call to an investigator about another woman who knew Jack, and who seemed just a little too cozy in her mannerisms toward him in the restaurant that night.

***

In the den of the mansion down the road, Gil showed Jack his notes and highlights on bank statements, and he explained to Jack what he had observed:

"I remembered that the thing that started this case was a phone call from the bank manager."

"Right."

"And the bank manager said that when he would call to inquire about suspicious charges, the pawns would always direct him to the same woman each time."

"Yes."

"So, I figured, there has to be some way of communicating with her other than through the mail, if something like that comes up unexpectedly.

"Uh, huh."

"So, I decided to stage a call from Clifford Williams about fraudulent activity on our account."

"Great idea! How did you do it?"

"Well, it's still in progress," Gil said, as he handed Jack a document. "I asked him to send me this fraud alert email which corresponds to the transactions I highlighted on this bank statement. They are the charges that we know Charlotte added. I left a note with one of my cash drops to Charlotte. It said: 'Bank manager asking about fraud. I asked him to call me back on my cell phone in two days at 3:00 p.m.' "

Jack spoke up, finishing Gil's reasoning, "And she already has your cell phone number from when she first inducted you into the crime ring, so that's good."

"Yes," Gil confirmed, "I also added this fraud alert email and corresponding bank statement, in with my note, to try to make her nervous enough to feel like she has to speak to the bank manager."

"When did you leave that note?"

"Two days ago."

"Excellent. So you think Charlotte should be calling you this afternoon with an instruction on how to forward the bank manager's call to her."

"Yes."

"That call will have to be longer than her usual coded messages. So, we'll be able to trace it."

"Exactly!"

"Great job, Gil!" said Jack with excited praise.

"And that's not all," Gil continued, "This time, I was able to follow the guy picking up the cash drop. After I ducked around the corner, I put on a big, long beard, like one of those hipsters from up north, and I changed my clothes to match the look. He had no clue it was me behind him, when he walked into a nearby FedEx/Kinkos."

"What did he do in there?"

"He sent a fax."

"Did you get the number?"

"Yes. It's a number in Monaco."

"Monaco. Damn it!"

"What?"

"That's a land without extradition."

"Will that mean a dead-end, if Charlotte's in Monaco?"

"Not necessarily. We may just have to travel to Monaco to lure the suspect over to France, after we've set a trap for her there."

"Once we figure out who she is."

"Yeah, once we figure out who she is."

***

Inside Venus' Bel Air mansion, behind the secret door through the wall of her master bedroom closet, Venus stood, as she listened to the investigator summarize his findings. Though her quick, sharp, mind understood exactly what he was reporting, the strong emotion of denial bellowed out of her:

"You idiot! I did not ask you to investigate her relationship with a man named Jack Wayne. I don't care what public servant she might be screwing! I asked you to investigate her relationship with a billionaire named Jack Smith! Now what are your findings about him!"

Unfazed by her anger or the insult, the investigator responded calmly but firmly: "There are no billionaires by the name of Jack Smith. Not in Texas. Not in California. Not anywhere in the United States. The man you asked about is not named Jack Smith. His name is Jack Wayne. He is not a billionaire. He is a senior Deputy District Attorney in Los Angeles, California. He is presumed to be the next District Attorney, when the current one retires."

The words "District Attorney" hung heavy in the air and rang in Venus' ears like the sound of a gun shot, shattering her denial into tiny pieces. Suddenly, Venus couldn't breathe. She hung up the phone, threw it into the pizza oven and slammed the metal door shut hard, as if burning the phone to smithereens could destroy the news she just heard: Jack Smith was Jack Wayne, Jack Wayne was Jack Smith. Panic and devastation simultaneously gripped her chest, as the room became darker and darker, and she struggled to breathe. The words barely squeaked out of her, as she spoke out loud the thing which she could not believe: "Jack Smith is Jack Wayne, Jack Wayne is Jack Smith." The room began spinning and Venus became weak. She realized she hadn't taken a breath since she heard those words. She gasped for air and fell to her knees grasping her chest. She repeated the words out loud, "Jack Smith is Jack Wayne, Jack Wayne is Jack Smith... Jack Smith is Jack Wayne. D--d--district attorney..."

One long deep breath to regain her strength, two long deep breaths, and a third, then Venus jumped to her feet as her sharp mind began to work fast. "He's onto me!" she exclaimed out loud. "I'm his target. I've been his prey this whole time!" Venus went wild behind her master room closet, opening file drawers as fast as she could, tearing out all the files she had compiled over decades, tossing them frantically into the pizza oven, burning every shred of paper in her vast files. She had no time, she had to move fast, faster than he could make his next move.

***

Two houses down the road, Jack instructed Gil to set a trap.

"It's after 3:00 and she hasn't called you yet. It must be because you're not fully 'in' the crime-ring yet. You're still being tested. However, she has spoken to Clifford before. Talking to him, is unavoidable because he's the bank manager where so many of her victims bank. She has to communicate with him to keep her game going. We already know that she is willing to stay on the phone longer with him. So, I want you to head over to the same place the cash carrier sent the fax, and send another one to the same number in Monaco. Say: 'Please call banker directly.' And give her Clifford's direct line.

I've already arranged to have his phone trace the call. When you send the fax, include the email and the bank statement that was with your note from your last cash drop so that she knows which account it's for."

Gil interrupted, "But won't she be suspicious of how I got that fax number?"

"No. she has no way of knowing that it's you sending the fax, instead of her cash carrier who is authorized to send faxes to that number."

***

An hour later, Venus jumped with a start at the sound of her old fax machine firing up. It left her heart beating as fast as if she had just sprinted a mile to escape danger. She closed the door to the pizza oven on the last shred of evidence that had to be destroyed; then she slowly, and as carefully as if she were approaching a wild animal, walked towards the fax machine. She lifted three pages from it, took a deep breath and walked over to her desk.

She sat at her desk, laid the papers down and paused. She sat comfortably in her chair before she began to read. When she did, the name on the bank statement popped out at her like it never had before. Suddenly, the letters J-A-K did not read like individual letters anymore; but instead, the bank account bearing the name JAK LLC, suddenly took on a very different phonetic sound. She stared at the paper and said the name out loud: "Jack."

Venus took in a long deep breath before she did another thing. She waited. She picked up her silver ballpoint pen and tapped it against the desk. Tap, tap, tap, tap. The sound went on, as she remembered wisdom from a long time ago. She was a very young child. She remembered her father teaching her that a master chess player never reacts quickly to his opponent's last move, but instead waits, and analyzes and strategizes every possible move on the board, any move that might be a reaction to the move he is considering, before he makes his next play. Venus waited. Tapping. Waiting to decide on her next play.

Then it came to her, clear as day. Jack would not have caused the fax to be sent, if he already had enough evidence to arrest her. The fax was bait. Venus burst into laughter, as tears of relief streamed down her face. "He does not have enough evidence!" she exclaimed aloud, as further tension-releiving laughter escaped her tightened lungs. It felt good to exhale, and to breathe again. She could breathe. She could wait. She could plot.

CHAPTER 27

Venus' shopping alibi would come in handy today. It would give her an opportunity to enter Jack's home while he was out. She would ask him to leave the door unlocked so that, upon his return, she could surprise him with something from a lingerie shop. She knew that such an enticing little promise would make Jack dismiss his assistant for the day, leaving her and Jack alone in Jack's Bel Air mansion. However, placing that phone call of temptation wasn't easy.

Venus picked up the phone and put it down three times before she was able to make the call, hyperventilating on each of the first three tries. Knowing the truth about Jack and that Jack knew the truth about her, complicated matters. It made Venus feel off balance and uncertain of her abilities.

It was imperative that she be very careful not to alert Jack to any changes in her demeanor towards him. She knew that her interactions with him must continue unchanged so as to leave him with the impression that he still had the upper hand. This meant, she was to play the part of gleeful, unsuspecting bride-to-be until her plan could be set in motion. Realizing the difficulty of the task, while her adrenaline still pumped fast from discovering Jack Wayne's true identity, Venus looked for something to calm her nerves.

Whisky was the answer. It was a beverage she hardly ever drank, except under extreme duress. It was quicker to calm the nerves than her usual wine or champagne. Venus walked over to a liquor cabinet she hadn't opened in years. Out of habit, she kept it locked, despite its safe location behind her secret door. Still shaking, Venus fumbled around for a silver key that glistened when it caught the light. She opened the cabinet door and reached for the most expensive bottle inside. It was a top shelf brand served in VIP lounges that host the world's royalty and billionaires. This one was from Dubai. She purchased it legitimately, albeit with stolen money from an English "client."

Still inside her secret room, now standing with a bottle of whisky in one hand, and a crystal tumbler in the other, Venus poured the whisky and placed the bottle on her desk. She then leaned against the desk to take her first long sip. She gulped it down and looked around at the shell of her headquarters, now emptied of all her tools of the trade; and Venus cursed herself for being such a fool as to fall in love.

With her second gulp of whisky, she looked over at the pizza oven feeling despair at the thought of her years' long work melted away in flames inside that oven. Her only solace was knowing that a handful of the biggest fish among her "clients" had been in her files for so long, that she now had their bank accounts memorized—every single digit.

Then, Venus took her third sip of whisky and cursed Jack Wayne. How dare he get the better of her! How dare he make her feel the way she did! *Feelings.* Jack had given Venus *feelings.* As the whisky coursed through her veins, Venus realized that Jack had never been her target the way men usually were. With Jack, it was *him* she wanted, not his money. The money was nothing but a distant afterthought, something that would ultimately be hers, but in a much less thrilling way than the money she earned for herself. Venus cursed herself for falling for a man so hard. The absurdity of it! For crying out loud! She hadn't even attempted to steal from a man she thought was a billionaire! Cursing and criticizing herself now, Venus narrowed her eyes with a thought that nagged her and mocked her—had she done so, she may have discovered his identity much sooner.

Gulping down her final shot of whisky, Venus then cursed Jack. She cursed him for being handsome, and charming, and sexy, and for using such weapons against her in a way she had done, against so many others. He bested her at her own game! Venus slammed the empty glass of whisky down hard on the table and she picked up the phone on that fourth and final attempt with rejuvenated feminine power. No man was going to best Venus at her own game.

***

Once inside Jack's Bel Air mansion, Venus roamed the vast upstairs hallway looking for signs of a room left unused. Now knowing that Jack's house was just a front, she also knew that he would not have a use for all of the many different rooms in the large home. She studied each room carefully, inspecting every lamp, coaster, chair, bed, bench, closet, desk, note pad, pen, and other knickknacks for any sign of use.

In one room, a notepad sitting on a desk had the first page missing. So, Venus closed that door as she exited, checking it off in her mind as unsuitable for her purposes.

In the next room, the remnants of a glass no longer present was evident from a ring left on a wood table without a coaster. Again, Venus closed the door and marked it off her mental list.

Finally, she saw a door that had promise. It was just far enough away from Jack's bedroom that he wouldn't find it handy. It was also too far from his assistant's quarters, whose room was on the first level of the house. The door that showed promise was on the right side of the hallway, meaning it faced the backyard—a place Jack would not be watching for the movements of a suspect he pursued. She surmised that Jack would only be using the rooms facing the street, or rooms with balconies that faced the direction of Venus' home.

So, the room Venus now eyed seemed the perfect candidate. The door was closed, which was a good sign. It suggested lack of use. Venus looked carefully at the granite floor in the hallway. She bent down for a closer look, hoping it hadn't been vacuumed in a few days. And she saw what she was looking for: dust. Judging from the dust accumulated in front of the door, undisturbed by footsteps, like the ones present in the dust in the middle of the hallway, running along a path from the staircase to Jack's bedroom and other rooms, Venus deduced that this room had not been used in awhile. She entered. She stopped in the entry way and saw a perfectly staged bedroom. The lamps weren't even plugged in. The chair was perfectly aligned and pushed in towards the small writing desk by the window overlooking the backyard. The closet was empty and not a single knickknack was left on any surfaces. The room appeared untouched since it's first staging. Venus decided this was the spot. The best chance she had of leaving a laptop in Jack's home, undiscovered, until after her plan rolled into motion, was to leave it right here in this room.

Venus stepped further inside, and closed the door behind her, as she began her work.

CHAPTER 28

Jack declined the bartender's offer of another beer and checked his watch anxiously. The usefulness of this country club, where he had spent so much time these past few months, had run its course. By now, Jack had already met every member, and managed to have Gil introduced to each of their assistants and other staff. Through Gil's savvy and charm, he created a social network among these staffers, which enabled him to identify which ones were Charlotte's pawns and which were not. Detective Jones had already run background checks on each of them and provided Gil and Jack with full reports that would be useful when the time came to make massive arrests. The only thing missing now was the link connecting these thieves to their ringleader. Therefore, Jack saw no more usefulness at this country club. The only reason he continued to frequent the place was to keep up appearances to enable Gil to continue socializing with the pawns, in order to seek any new information that might reveal the ring leader.

Feeling bored by the lack of his opportunity to gain additional leads, Jack checked his watch again, anxious for the place he'd rather be. The enticing little promise that Venus gave him over the phone occupied his mind. He kept wondering what color she picked for that lingerie she had teased him with during her call. Did she pick white to signal a path towards exchanging nuptials? Or did she pick royal blue to match her eyes—those eyes that kept Jack so captivated, and even speechless sometimes. As he sipped his last beer, Jack's mind wandered on. Now, he pictured Venus in red lingerie. He liked seeing Venus in red, especially when she wore bright red lipstick. His mind's eye moved along Venus' extraordinary body, barely covered with teasing lingerie, silk and lace, barely there calling for Jack to tear it off of her, ... with his teeth, maybe? Jack smiled wide and gulped down the last bit of his beer. He placed a $10 bill on the bar and hurried towards the door. Completely oblivious to Venus' true intentions, Jack decided he had given her enough time to prepare to receive him.

***

Pulling into the drive of his fake Bel Air mansion, Jack parked his blue Bugatti, courtesy of LAPD's impound lot, next to Venus' stolen blue Bugatti.

He slammed the door and almost sprinted towards the house, eager for Venus' surprise. He stopped at the door, caught his breathe and gathered up a cool demeanor. He twisted the unlocked door knob and was made instantly breathless by what awaited him inside. Venus stood at the top of the staircase, entirely nude, except for a few dangling diamonds, off her earlobes, her neck and her wrists, and the straps of her barely there stiletto heels. Her smooth dark hair was pinned up in an elegant updo with moe sparkling hair pins - also made of diamonds. Jack closed the door behind him, and unthinking, slowly walked towards the mesmerizing beauty.

The bright red lipstick starkly contrasted against her milky white skin, dark hair and bright blue eyes captivated him even more than his fantasies of her moments ago. As he climbed the steps, the sparkle from her diamond bracelets drew his eyes downward. They were linked together, binding her hands together in front of her nude body. That body. Tall and slender with curves in exactly the right places, Jack's eyes caressed every inch of it. Then the two diamond bracelets, bound by a string of diamonds, sparkled again and caught his eye when Venus moved ever so slightly and said: "Take me in, Jack. I've been a bad girl."

Handcuffs! Sparkling, diamond *hand-cuffs!* Jack rushed up the stairs now and swooped Venus up into his arms, carrying her right passed the closed door, behind which a planted laptop hid; and he blazed into his bedroom, dropping Venus on the soft feather bed. He climbed on top of her, unable to stem his desire. He ravished her with kisses, first all over her face, then all over her neck, then down her chest, around her bosom, then down her waist, past her bound hands, as he gently spread her legs apart with his strong hands, and buried his face in between. Venus gasped in ecstasy and Jack took her, jut as she had asked him to. He devoured her womanhood claiming it as his, all his, until her cries of ecstasy grew louder and louder, until she could hardly breathe. Jack lifted his head, and let his hands go to work as he watched Venus wreathe and turn, her head thrown back, and her hands still bound with diamonds. He watched, and tickled and tantalized her, then pressed his fingers in deep until she burst with pleasure and her whole body began to shake. He indulged in the sight and the sound of her keeping his fingers relentless until he was sure her long climax began to subside. Ever so gently, and slowly, he removed his fingers, placed one last gentle kiss between her legs then lifted her still bound hands above her head. He gently lay on top of her, still fully clothed, and nestled in comfortably, now gently kissing her face, listening to her breathing, as he waited for her to catch her breathe. Then he whispered in her ear, "Rest a little longer dear, before it's my turn." All Venus could do was smile. He left her without any more energy than that. As her breathing began to slow, Jack unlatched the diamond chain that bound her wrists, then slowly undressed himself.

When Venus' breathe finally became regular, he pressed himself inside her, taking and delivering pure pleasure and bliss.

***

After several more rounds of pleasure and ecstasy, Venus wrapped her arms and legs around Jack in a tight grip and began whispering things she truly felt, but didn't mean. She said the things she would have said, if his name was really Jack Smith, Bel Air billionaire, and not Jack Wayne, Chief Deputy District Attorney.

"Let's get married now, Jack, let's not wait. We could elope in Europe, honeymoon in France, or Italy or a Greek island."

The word Europe reluctantly drew Jack's mind back to his investigation. He didn't want to think of work now. He just wanted to indulge in this moment with Venus.

"Nevermind the future, Venus. Let's enjoy right now."

Venus gripped him tighter with her legs and nipped at his ear, then whispered, "Please, Jack, Please."

"We can't plan our wedding yet, Venus. There's a lot I have to tell you first."

Venus' eyebrows shot up at the shocking statement. What was he going to tell her? She kept her composure and delicately asked him: "What, darling?"

"I can't tell you just yet. I have some business I have to wrap up first."

"Business?" Venus repeated as her sharp mind went into overdrive. "How long will this business take to wrap up?"

"I'm not sure."

"A few months? A few weeks? Do you have an estimate?"

Jack sighed, "Not really. One thing depends on another."

"But how close are you, Jack?"

Jack lifted his head and looked into Venus' eyes. She panicked. Did she give herself away? Her heart began to race and her eyes darted back and forth. Jack stared into her blue eyes trying to read her thoughts. She could feel his gaze burrowing into her. She had to regain control, but she couldn't, her heart was racing and panic was rising.

"Venus," Jack said. "Don't be angry. I'm not evading marriage. I just need a little more time."

"Oh!" Venus sighed with relief. "Angry. I'm not angry at you Jack." Venus flashed her best smile and gave him her most enchanting laugh.

Jack began to laugh with her. "What a relief," he said, "I thought you were about to tear my head off. You looked really upset."

"Never! Jack!" Venus gleamed with the joy of still being on top. "I could never be angry at you," the smooth seductive vixen charmed him even further, "Maybe I was just a little scared, that you might run away from me!" she lied coyly.

Jack gave Venus a long passionate kiss, as he held her strong in his arms, and said between breaths, "You'll never have to worry about that!"

He said it with such sincerity that Venus' heart believed every bit of it, but her mind warned her, "stick to the plan."

Venus ran her fingers in Jack's thick brown hair as she returned his passionate kiss, and she wished, for a moment, that the words between them were true. When she spoke, her mind took over, and she continued according to plan.

"Jack, even if we can't get married. Come away with me! Let's have a honeymoon anyway, even if we won't officially marry until a later date. That way, I won't have to nag you about a wedding date, and you can take your time finishing your business." She stopped short of asking him again for a timeline. She couldn't risk asking any questions that might tip him off that she was trying to gauge how far along he was in his investigation of her. The wheels of her plan were already in motion, so it was unnecessary to press the question. All she had to do now, was to get him to come along.

Jack took a long time to answer. His mind seemed a million miles away. She watched his face carefully trying to gauge his expression for any sign at all of what he was thinking. She found him unreadable. A better poker player than her! Venus knew that every minute longer that she indulged in Jack's company, she was playing with fire.

Finally, he spoke, "Europe is nice this time of year. I might have a little business in Switzerland." It was a stupid statement. Despite Jack's complete oblivion to who Venus really was, he should not have named a place key to his investigation.

Hearing that one word, "Switzerland," Venus knew there was no time to waste—and no mercy to be given.

So, she pressed. Testing her leverage and gauging her time, Venus asked: "Can we stop in London, first? My favorite shops are in London."

Jack smiled. He saw no harm in taking a short detour for vacation purposes, before resuming his investigation near Switzerland. Still believing Venus was the same, sweet, elegant, perfect woman he had met six months ago, Jack easily answered, "yes" to Venus' plotted request.

CHAPTER 29

While Jack and Venus traveled to London, Venus' brother, Victor, was hard at work. The one and only person in the world who Venus ever trusted, was the one she called from Bel Air, the day she learned of Jack's identity. It was a quick call with a coded message: "Send our favorite stallion out to pasture."

The message sent her brother into high gear. He rushed to complete all the tasks necessary to arrange for a quick departure from London, and an even faster liquidation of all assets in Dubai. The liquidation also included the contents of Venus' house in Bel Air, and her stolen blue Bugatti, which would be en route to Dubai, before Jack spent his first night in London.

Much like Venus, Victor had his own pawns. All of them delivery men, expert at disguising themselves as movers, cleaning and clearing out spaces without leaving a trace behind, and swiftly loading goods onto shipping containers. Victor had a team in every major port. This time, his Southern California team, worked its magic from Bel Air to Long Beach, California.

Victor worked fast, having pre-sold these items before their arrival in Dubai. Their friend who owned the Dubai warehouse, where Venus stored her goods, was a willing taker and knew where to send the money. Never having committed any crimes in Dubai, Venus and her brother were safe from detection there. The liquidation looked legitimate, would never raise suspicion by the warehousemen or local authorities, and therefore, transfers to Swiss bank accounts, were safe, swift and easy. It was the safest and fastest way for Venus and Victor to enter retirement. The liquidation was easy. One warehouse owner in Dubai considered the lump sum price of all their goods a bargain.

More difficult, was the liquidation of a yacht in Port Hucle. A long-standing customer, who Venus and Victor frequently served in Dubai, was interested; but, he would not be available for another week or two.

However, the most important task left to Venus' brother, was the paperwork—very important paperwork, which required the smooth charm that only a master con-artist, even more advanced than Venus, could achieve.

For this, Venus' brother, Victor, called upon his oldest and most naive friend. It was the manager of a bank branch in London, who had performed many favors for Victor over the years, believing that Victor was a quirky, eccentric, intensely private billionaire. The bank manager had a reputation of impeccable integrity. He was above reproach. That was the very reason Victor had targeted him so many years ago. It began with a friendship, in which Victor played the role of eccentric billionaire afraid of international banks, large corporations, and strangers. Little by little, he allowed the bank manager to court his business. The bank manager frequently invited Victor to tea, then lunch, then dinner—where each time, the bank manager would try to persuade Victor to trust his bank branch with Victor's money.

Victor drug the charade along for an entire year, before finally agreeing to begin opening accounts at the bank manager's branch to deposit some of Victor's money, but only under strict conditions, which included the bank manager agreeing to serve as Victor's personal banking concierge—who would bring the bank to Victor, instead of requiring Victor to go to the bank. This meant, anything that had to be signed, the bank manager would bring to Victor. It also meant, that any cash deposits or withdrawals, would be delivered to, and on behalf of, Victor by the personal hand of the bank manager. The concierge service came with a fee, of course. A small $10,000 fee each month, plus $1,000 cash per transaction, paid in cash directly to the bank manager. He was thrilled to be of service. Little did the bank manager know, that Victor's sole purpose, was to avoid being seen on the bank's security cameras, and that the vast sums of money that Victor deposited over the years, was all stolen money.

This time, it was the signing of a bank signature card that was most imperative. That, and several very large wire transfers. The sensitive nature of this project required the utmost secrecy and cooperation from Victor's trusted personal concierge.

CHAPTER 30

Detective Jones shifted in his uncomfortable seat. He hated the stupid chairs used at these conferences. The cushion of the seats only stayed comfortable for the first few hours, of the first day. Today was the third day, and approaching the final presentation. It had been a long and uninteresting conference, and he was glad he had ultimately decided to identify his status as "retired" when he had registered for the conference. That resulted in fewer questions from new people wanting to know what case he was working on now. It also meant his phone wouldn't ring so much. Between Sarah Cartwright and Jack Wayne, Detective Jones had his hands full. After this conference, he was headed straight to Europe to help Sarah research obscure stories about unsung heroes of WWII, for Sarah's next historical fiction novel. He would start in London and meet her in Normandy, actually, off the coast of Normandy.

Detective Jones had contemplated skipping this last session of the conference. He stayed only because the conference usually saved the most interesting unsolved cases for the last session. It was carefully timed to give food for thought just before the group was let out to mingle at cocktail hour. In years' past, detectives from different jurisdictions discovered links between their cases across the country that helped catch a criminal who left clues in different places, which alone were insufficient to make a case, but together could solve a case. Thus, it became a tradition that this time-slot presented the most perplexing or interesting unsolved case. That was the reason Detective Jones reluctantly stayed for the last session.

As he waited for the next speaker to take the podium and set up his presentation, Detective Jones busied himself with thoughts he sketched out an a notepad where he outlined his "To Do" list for when he would first arrive in London. "Twin-engine helicopter" was the first thing written down. Detective Jones had his pilot's license and wanted to put in a few hours of flying before rolling up his sleeves and digging through old newspaper clippings and other library materials and public records for Sarah. More than just a joy ride, the helicopter was also necessary for the next step of his research with Sarah, which included an air tour of the setting of her novel. As Detective Jones jotted down more “to do” items, his attention was suddenly drawn back to the conference at the sound of an uproar of hooting, hollering and whistling. It was a surprising sound, given that it arose in a room full of detectives awaiting the speech of an insurance fraud investigator. Like Detective Jones, many of the conference attendees had contemplated skipping it, out of a belief that a discussion of insurance fraud couldn't be that interesting.

Now, this sudden unexpected uproar from the crowd peaked his interest. When Detective Jones looked up, he saw what all the commotion was about. Displayed on a large screen behind the speaker was a woman of extraordinary beauty. In large letters, the title: "Lady Bad Luck" appeared above the photo. The photo seemed a little inappropriate, because it only showed the woman from the neck down, which had the effect of inviting a room mostly filled with macho men to indulge in the sight of the woman's body. She was tall and slender, with mouth watering curves. Her long blonde hair was softly curled at the ends, and seemed to wrap itself gently around her breasts. The tight but elegant dress she wore turned the men in the room into apes. When they finally calmed down, the speaker explained himself.

"Our lawyers advised us not to show her face, lest she sue us for defamation."

Laughter erupted from the crowd.

"This is no laughing matter, gentlemen. This woman might be responsible for the disappearance of millions and millions of dollars in luxury goods."

"Show us her face!" one man shouted from the crowd.

"We cannot do that."

"Why not!" he taunted.

"Because, we don't have any evidence against her."

"Awwww," the crowd booed, which was quickly interrupted by one heckler who called out, "So strip search her!"

The boos turned to cheers, and the speaker shifted nervously at the podium before he thought of a quick come back, "We can't get a warrant for that."

The crowd laughed, but another nay sayer heckled the speaker further. "Why is she up there, if you have no evidence?" he hollered.

"You know these insurance guys," a different man replied, "they'll say anything to get out of paying on an insurance claim."

The crowd laughed again.

Detective Jones stood up and addressed the rowdy crowd, "Come on, guys, give him a chance. Let's hear what he has to say. I mean, he was kind enough to show us her picture, wasn't he?"

The crowd cheered again, then a few seconds later, settled down. Detective Jones nodded to the speaker and the speaker mouthed, "thank you," to Detective Jones.

With the crowd settled, the speaker resumed his presentation.

"We call her Lady Bad Luck because her mere presence seems to cause things to disappear. In the Middle Eastern culture, they would blame the evil eye. She looks at something that she covets, then soon afterward, something bad happens to it.

"But I am not superstitious. Far too often, after Lady Bad Luck is seen in a luxury retail store, an item she appeared to be interested in would go missing. It took many years for our investigators to notice this pattern. At first, we believed that she was working with the retail stores who were presenting us with false claims. But we could never find a link between her and any employee of these stores—not a manger, not a salesperson, not a stock room or delivery employee, nobody.

"However, her presence at these stores, just before a loss event is claimed by our insured, happens too frequently for it to be mere coincidence; and it happens in too many places. In this photograph, she is inside Harrods in London. From what you can see in this picture, she is a blonde." The speaker clicked a button and a new picture appeared on the screen, "But here, at this Versace store in Italy, she is a redhead." The speaker clicked a button again, displaying the same woman from behind. "And here, she is at a jewelry counter at Saks Fifth Avenue in New York, where she is a brunette. Only the keen eye of one of our best investigators noticed her face and realized it was the same woman at each of these locations, where the insured made a claim over goods lost or stolen, soon after Lady Bad Luck inspected the item, but made no purchase."

As the speaker continued his presentation, clicking through various photos of the woman in various retail stores across the world, Detective Jones studied each photograph, wondering what seemed so familiar about the woman. Although each shot was a still shot taken from video surveillance at each store, he could see something familiar about the woman's movement. He could almost imagine her gait, as she walked. There was something familiar about how she carried herself—very elegant, very poised—so much so that each still shot, from candid video footage of the woman shopping, seemed to capture her in a beautiful pose. The woman always posed as she walked, or stood in place, or reached for a garment, as if knowing she were on display and people were watching; as if inviting them to watch as she mesmerized the onlooker. She was a captivating woman indeed, and Detective Jones couldn't shake the feeling that he had seen her somewhere before.

The speaker continued showing various photographs of Lady Bad Luck, as he explained: "A series of coincidences will never lead us anywhere. That is why we asked for this slot in this year's conference so that we can show you various photographs of the woman, in the event you recognize something from one of your cases, where a luxury item was reported lost or stolen.

Please observe her clothing, her jewelry, her shoes, her handbags, anything she is wearing for a clue that might connect to one of your cases.

"For example, in this photograph, it is believed that everything she is wearing, except for her ring, is stolen property. The dress appears to be a one of a kind high-end designer dress that somehow never made its way to the customer that bought it. We know it left the store for delivery to the customer, but the customer adamantly denied ever receiving it. The customer sued the store for her money back, and that's when the store called us to make an insurance claim. Everything about the dress that Lady Bad Luck is wearing in this photograph, is identical to the one of a kind designer dress that went missing—right down to the golden zipper up the side, and the beading down the neckline—except for one thing. Lady Bad Luck has modified the dress, with only one change, she added a slit up the right side of the leg.

"Of course, our lawyers tell us we could never prove that; but we say, it's far too coincidental, especially because the handbag and shoes are the same brand and same design of items that disappeared in the same fashion, from a different store, after an attempted delivery to a different customer, who has no connection to the customer who never received that dress. Still, our lawyers say, those shoes and that dress are sold in various retail stores around the world, so no cigar. We can't pin anything on her."

Detective Jones stared at one object in the photograph. It was a sparkling blue gem stone on the left hand of the woman in the photograph. It was just as familiar as the woman's body and her pose. But the presenter had said the ring was not stolen, so Detective Jones dismissed it from being a possible clue in one of his cases. Nonetheless, he raised his hand to ask the speaker a question.

"Have you been able to identify her, through her purchases?"

"No," answered the speaker, "She is only a window-shopper, she has never made a purchase at any of these stores."

"Oooohhhh," the crowd gave a collective suspicion-filled response.

"I'm glad you're beginning to see things my way," the speaker replied, triumphantly. "We almost had a lead involving a luxury automobile, but that turned out to be a dead-end."

The conference moderator held up a 30 second warning sign to indicate to the speaker that it was time to wrap up the presentation. The speaker then concluded:

"Now, hopefully, you'll take a more careful look at the materials that are being passed around. You will find a list of all the insurance claims we've investigated where we saw video surveillance footage of Lady Bad Luck appearing inside our insured's store within a week of the loss event. The list includes the date of loss, the date Lady Bad Luck appeared at the store, and a description and photograph of the lost or stolen item. The most recent event is the one that helped me convince the conference organizers to allow me to make this presentation in this time slot today. It's because Lady Bad Luck herself is the one who drove off the lot with the allegedly stolen Bugatti. We did not pay this insurance claim due to the sheer stupidity of the salesman, who allowed her to drive off the lot without even asking for identification. He thought the wire confirmation meant the car was already paid for, nullifying any need to ask her for I.D. From what we can see on the video, the fool was just too enamored with her to follow ordinary procedure, or to even notice that the LLC that paid for the car has no identifiable owners who could answer for the wire reversal, which apparently occurred less than an hour after she drove off the lot."

A member of the audience piped up, "Sounds like a civil matter."

"Yes. We expected the police to say that," replied the speaker, "But this was our first and only direct link between Lady Bad Luck and a stolen item. After purportedly purchasing the vehicle, Lady Bad Luck claimed to have driven it back to the dealership, after business hours, where it must've been stolen off the street, she insisted, if the dealership didn't find it there in the morning. Although the vehicle was stolen from a dealership in Beverly Hills, Lady Bad Luck gave an address in Orange County, which turned out to be nothing but a post office box for an empty shell of an LLC."

Detective Jones flipped through the materials and saw a picture of a blue Bugatti that looked almost identical to the one Jack had been driving out of LAPD's impound lot. Because he had a plane to catch, Detective Jones didn't have time to stay and ask the speaker any more questions about that case. He figured a phone call to the impound lot would produce more information, anyhow. Detective Jones flipped open his notepad, and added one more item at the bottom of his "To Do" list: "Blue Bugatti - found out how impound got it."

CHAPTER 31

Venus and Jack had been in London for three days, where they enjoyed the finest parts of the city, including elegant galas, a Shakespeare play, and fine dining. While Venus entertained Jack, her brother was hard at work.

Relying on their long-standing friendship and business relationship, Victor asked his English personal concierge at the London branch of an American bank to perform one small, but very valuable, favor. He asked the bank manager to open an account before receiving the signature cards from the account holder. Victor had explained to the bank manager that it was urgent. His American friend was en route to London to consummate a billion dollar business deal for a conglomerate that would receive millions of dollars from various initial investors before the American could arrive in London.

Victor promised the bank manager that he would deliver original signatures, and a copy of the account owner's photo I.D., and all other necessary forms, signed in blue ink, as soon as the friend arrived in London, but that it was imperative that the bank account be open and active and receiving wire transfers before the business man's arrival.

The bank manager was eager to help, and accommodated Victor's request.

That occurred exactly three days ago—just before Victor had embarked on a whirlwind of a trip. On that trip, he had met his second most naive friend, in the form of yet another personal banking concierge, similar to the one he had in London—but at a different bank, in a different country, with stricter financial privacy laws, near the Swiss border. He met the gentleman to receive a very important delivery, traveled into Switzerland with that delivery, then returned to London for his final and most important task.

Now, it was time to obtain original signatures from the American business man, whose new bank account had already received many millions of dollars in wire transfers during the past three days.

Victor entered the luxury hotel through the staff's entrance, and silently walked up the back stairs. He gave a gentle tap on Venus' door and patiently waited.

She was inside the Presidential suite, which was filled with luxury finishes—marble floors, and intricately carved pillars, which lined a long room, so large it could host a small, intimate ball. But this was not the door he knocked on. He knocked on the door of the adjoining room, where Venus answered, and ushered him into the Presidential Suite from a private door inside the adjoining room. Victor entered cautiously, carefully hiding himself by the pillar closest to the door.

In the distance, Victor could see a well dressed man, sunken deep into a brown leather armchair, who stared strangely at the glass of red wine he held in his hand. The man seemed to be debating with, or at, the wine glass. Victor handed Venus the important papers, exchanging only a few quick words, before Victor ducked completely behind the pillar, trying to stand outside of the man's view.

Victor was too curious to stay completely hidden. For, it was hard not to watch the man, who made funny faces after every sip of wine, and stared pointedly at his wine glass as if it held the answer to an unsolved mystery.

Venus soon came back with the forms entirely filled in, by the man's own hand. As the man rubbed his head, as if in pain, Venus suddenly announced, "Jack, Darling, you forgot to sign this one." She walked purposefully towards Jack, placed the paper beneath his pen and demanded with one word, "Sign," and Jack did.

Upon her return, she handed Victor the papers and said, "Don't worry, he won't remember any of this in the morning."

CHAPTER 32

Detective Jones' tray table was down. His right arm rested on the tray table, with his hand wrapped around a half-drank whisky on the rocks. He always flew on the red-eye when crossing the Atlantic because he liked to sleep through his flights. In his younger days, he would use dark beer to do the trick; but, recently, he discovered that whisky puts him to sleep faster. While his right hand lay loosely around the whisky glass, his head leaned against the window as he snored lightly.

As he slept, visions of a beautiful woman filled his dreams. He saw the curve of her body. Though slender and tall, she was still dangerously curvy in just the right places. Her long red nails rested at the bend of her delicate waist. Though she stood still, her bent knee on one side, and popped hip on the other promised the seductive movement of a woman in motion, swinging her hips as she walked. The woman stood behind a floor to ceiling window dazzling in the sunlight. The blue ring sparkling on her hand, raised Detective Jone's eyes upwards to a beautiful face, with even bluer eyes. They were striking blue eyes. Unforgettable eyes. They blessed a face so beautiful, it had made Detective Jones say, "Jack, you lucky dog, you."

Detective Jones' eyes popped open as he involuntarily exclaimed: "Jack's lady friend!" The woman in the photograph—Lady Bad Luck—was the woman Detective Jones had seen standing in Jack's window. Vivid memory came rushing back to him. Two blue Bugattis. Both sitting in Jack's driveway. One from the impound lot, and one with temporary dealership plates. It was her! It had to be her!

Detective Jones, reached into his pants pocket, then remembered that his cell phone was in his carry-on luggage, in the overhead bin. He stood quickly almost knocking the whisky off the tray table. He grabbed it before it spilled on the passenger who was asleep in the seat next to him. He thought of climbing past him, but the passenger in the aisle seat was also asleep. Then heavy turbulence began and Detective Jones fell back into his own seat. He hated turbulence. It always made him dizzy. He laid his head against the seat and closed his eyes. Damn this turbulence. He would wait. After landing, he would deplane and make all the necessary phone calls. Several hours remained before he would reach his destination.

CHAPTER 33

Gil was feeling antsy. He hadn't received an instruction from Charlotte in far too long. Longer than usual. She typically ordered him to make cash drops every few days. Yet, two weeks had gone by without a word.

Out of sheer boredom, feeling useless, and not really expecting to find anything, Gil logged on to the online banking portal of the account their investigation was using to lure Charlotte towards them. What he saw shocked him.

The last transaction was an outgoing wire of all funds. The balance left in the account was $0.00. Before he could even begin to comprehend this, he heard banging on the door. He jumped out of his seat in the den and ran towards the front door. It was Beth. She was frantic, panicked and crying. She was blubbering unintelligibly.

"I'm in so much trouble! I'm in so much trouble! I can't believe this is happening," she carried on.

Gil tried to calm her down and directed her towards the living room. "Beth, I'm busy right now. What is it?"

"I can't ... huh, . . . I just can't . . " She cried, as black eye makeup ran down her face. "I never would've done this. I never would've agreed. I thought it was just a little off the top. Something nobody would ever notice."

"Notice what Beth?"

"The money."

A sinking feeling dropped in Gil's stomach. "What money Beth. Please calm down. I'm having my own emergency. I need you to calm down so you can explain."

"My boss' money. I think it's Charlotte. But she's never done this before. She's only ever taken a little at a time. Now there's millions of dollars missing. My boss is going crazy. I heard him yelling downstairs. He was cussing at his banker. Someone wired millions of dollars out of his account."

Gil began to realize what was happening. Charlotte must be making a grand finale. A large foul swoop to end a long crime spree. This was their last chance to catch her. He had to get Beth out of there fast so he could dispatch subpoenas and make several phone calls. All his attempts to get Beth to leave were to no avail.

Beth wailed, "Where will I go?! I can't go back to my boss' house or my apartment. I'll probably get arrested."

"Ok. Fine. You can stay here, just go in the back yard. I won't let anyone in. I need some privacy right now."

"uh, oh... ohh.. ok," she managed to utter through her bawling.

Gil showed Beth to the backyard bar and told her to help herself. He then went inside and locked the door so she couldn't come in. He went back to the den and locked that door too.

He immediately called the bank to try to gain information about the wire.

"This is urgent. A large sum has been wired without authorization. You need to act quickly in obtaining all information you can about the receiving bank. I need to know the name of the account holder, the name of the receiving bank and the address of the bank branch. I'm a police officer with LAPD. I believe the receiving bank account is being used for grand larceny. You must act quickly in cooperating with me and in gaining the cooperation of the receiving bank. We will have subpoenas out and an order to freeze the account as quickly as you provide me the initial information I've requested."

After ending his call with the bank, Gil made several calls to the direct line of Sam Chapman, a Senior Deputy District Attorney who Gil knew could get things done in a snap. When all his calls went unanswered, he realized that he'd been using his cover cell phone. So, he ran upstairs, unlocked a fireproof safe in his secondary office, and removed his real cell phone. He saw 15 missed calls from Detective Jones. So he called him first.

"Where they hell are you guys?" Detective Jones answered, "I've been trying to get ahold of you for hours! Longer, actually, since last night!"

"Sorry, I've been using my cover phone."

"Well, there's something you need to know about Jack's lady friend."

"Who?"

"You know, that drop-dead gorgeous woman who visits him in that Bel Air mansion."

"Venus?"

"Yeah, she sure looks like a Venus."

"No. That's her name, Venus."

"Oh. That's fitting. Well, what I want you to know is that she's on the radar of insurance investigators as a possible international thief."

As the detective said this, Gil paced down the hall and walked into a spare bedroom that neither he nor Jack had ever used. It had a view of the backyard and he wanted to check on Beth. But something else caught his attention. Sitting on the small desk by the window was a laptop, open and turned on. Gil walked slowly towards it as he absent-mindedly said to the detective: "Tell me more."

Gil saw one long black hair dangling on the seat of the chair at the desk. He picked it up and whispered, "Venus."

"Yeah, that's who I'm talking about," said the Detective as he continued describing what he learned at the conference. Gil listened while browsing through the laptop. Screen shots of wire confirmations transferring millions of dollars from various accounts were saved in the photos. The account into which all wires were made was the same.

As the Detective spoke, Gil suddenly remembered the moment he almost crashed into a moving van hours after Venus and Jack left the country. Still holding the phone to his ear, he bolted down the stairs, and out the door, as he ran to Venus' house. He stood peering through the window of the bare and empty home, as Detective Jones continued to describe what he learned at the conference. The Detective ended by saying: "What are the chances that you guys are hunting for one thief, but draw in another?"

Gil's voice was ominous, as he answered, "None."

"None? Oh, there's some chance, isn't there?"

"No," Gil said adamantly, "Venus is Charlotte."

Just then, Gil's cover phone rang in his pocket. Hold on Detective, I have to take this.

Gil put the second phone to his other ear. Detective Jones could hear only Gil's side of the conversation. The call was from the bank. Upon answering, Gil heard the pleasant voice of a helpful lady: "Everything is under control, officer. We have the name and social security number of the individual on the account. The bank is an American bank with a branch in London. The account was opened in the London branch. We have put a hold on the account and alerted the London authorities. The individual's name is Jack Wayne."

"Jack Wayne!" Gil screamed, nearly breaking the eardrums of both his listeners.

"Jack Wayne? he repeated, incredulously. Did I hear you correctly? Did you say Jack Wayne or did you say Jack Smith?"

"Jack Wayne, sir. We have his social security number. The London authorities say he entered London through customs, showing his passport there. He will be caught."

Gil hung up on the bank and screamed into Detective Jones' ear, "Jack's in London with Charlotte! And she knows who he is! She's framing him for her crimes! In London!"

"I'm in London too! But I'm in the air! Give me his cover phone number. I'll try to reach him. Also, where's he staying?"

CHAPTER 34

Jack was in the Presidential suite of a luxury hotel in the heart of London. He wanted to eat breakfast in his bathrobe but Venus had insisted that he get dressed. It was an odd request, because they had lounged in their bathrobes for breakfast on each morning before that; but today, she was adamant and insistent, and almost a nag about it, so he got up to get dressed, as the room service butler laid out the table.

Once dressed, he came out of the bedroom to find unwelcome guests. Three uniformed police officers stood between him and the front door.

"Can I help you officers?"

"Yes. You can give us your passport," said one police officer.

"And come with us," said another.

"I'm afraid there must be some mistake," Jack said, confused.

"No mistake. We recognize you from footage at the airport," said the third officer, "Your name is Jack Wayne, correct?"

Just then, the cell phone in Jack's hand pinged twice, two text messages from Gil read:

"V. is Charlotte!"

"Get out of Dodge! V. is Charlotte!"

Jack looked at Venus, who stood to one side, with a look of regret and immeasurable guilt. She shook her head, as her blue eyes became watery and she whispered, "I'm so sorry, Jack. Please forgive me. It had to be done."

In an instant, Jack understood exactly what was happening.

The officers advanced towards him, announcing that he was under arrest for being so bold as to steal from: "his royal highness' closest friend." Instinctively, Jack fought. He had no faith in a system he knew nothing about. The mention of wronged royalty fueled his resistance more vehemently. It was an alarming reminder of the only thing he was certain of—that this country's due process would look nothing like his own. So, he was quick, and fierce, and he capitalized on the element of surprise.

Years of kickboxing used solely for staying fit, suddenly served as his saving grace. Jack leapt in the air and spun around faster than the advancing officers could react. His foot struck one in the face, whose head knocked heads with the one next to him and they both tumbled to the ground unconscious. One strong right hook to the third, sent him falling down hard. All three were out cold. Jack looked around the room wildly as he heard more officers clamoring up the hall towards his door. Then, guidance came from an unlikely source. Venus shouted, desperately: "The fire escape Jack, the fire escape!"

Jack's eyebrows furrowed in confusion. *Is she for real!? She just framed me and is now advising my escape?* With no time to ponder the absurdity, Jack bolted for the window and ran down the fire escape. Police were parked just below. He barely escaped their grasp and ran as fast as he could. His cell phone was buzzing angrily in the pocket of his lapel, but he couldn't stop now to check it.

***

With three officers unconscious and more officers imminently near, Venus slipped through a door to a connecting suite. The connected suite had been reserved in a different name altogether. Not even hotel staff new she had the key to the adjoining door. Now safely outside the suspicion of officers pursuing Jack, Venus peered out the window and watched Jack darting between cars, ducking below awnings, and barely escaping the reach of pursuing officers. Guilt gripped Venus' heart as she watched the horror of Jack being hunted like an animal. She felt a desperate urge to assist his escape, but didn't how. A thought came to her, just before embarking on her own escape route. She picked up the telephone of the hotel suite and called a number she had memorized recently. It was the new pawn who had been faxing the bank statements of JAK LLC. When Gil answered, Venus spoke quickly: "The police are pursuing your friend near Harrods in London." She then hung up the phone and continued her own course.

***

Jack could hear the helicopters buzzing above him as he darted through traffic, to evade pursuing police officers, he tried to get out of sight of the police in the air by ducking under awnings, running inside buildings, then out their back doors, and sprinting through the streets as fast as he could.

***

Gil quickly made a desperate call to Detective Jones, "Have you landed yet?"

"No, I'm still in the air."

"On a plane?"

"No, a helicopter, I'm a little busy now Gil, I'll call you back."

"Wait!" Gil screamed . . .

***

Jack sprinted through the streets of London, zigzagging through people and cars. He looked behind him to gauge the distance between him and pursuing officers. Out in the open now, the damned helicopters were still buzzing over him. Damn! He just couldn't loose them! His phone kept pinging in his lapel and he kept running. This time he missed the curb and tripped. His cell phone flew out of his lapel pocket, and his cell phone screen lit up with another text. He now saw a series of texts:

"Look up! D. Jones"

"Look up! Look up!"

"D. Jones in air!!"

As Jack saw these texts, he suddenly became aware of the distinction between the helicopters in the sky. He had assumed they were both chasing him, and kept evading the sound, ducking under awnings trying to get them to lose sight of him. But he now saw that only one was a police helicopter. The other came screeching towards him. It was close enough now that he could see Detective Jones in the pilot seat. Jack stood and ran towards it, seeing a rope hanging down. Jack leapt for the rope but missed. He leapt again and caught it this time, with one hand.

He dangled by his right arm trying to reach up with his left arm but the wind was too strong. He twisted his body, swinging with all his body weight a hard twist with all the force he could muster as he swung his free arm up and finally caught the rope. He now had a firm grasp with both hands. "Hold on tight, Jack! They're shooting at us, I have to get out of range," he heard Detective Jones holler. Jack looked down to see the pursing officers with their weapons drawn. "Keep both hands tight, Jack!" he heard the detective holler again, as the helicopter rose up into the air and took a hard left turn. The rope swung Jack around and he twirled in the air like a whirlpool in the wind. He clasped the rope with his knees and ankles and held tight with both hands until Detective Jones brought the helicopter to a hover above an office building that shielded him from the police on the ground. When the rope finally became steady, Jack used his strong arms to climb up the rope and into the helicopter. Exhausted, he fell back and moved away from the open door, knowing he didn't have the strength to pull it shut. He buckled in the seat furthest from the opening, and Detective Jones took off like a bullet headed for the English Channel.

The police helicopter followed in hot pursuit.

"Can they cross the Channel?" Detective Jones hollered back at Jack.

"I don't know! I think the UK left the EU, it must be out of their jurisdiction!"

"Well, we're heading to France, so I guess we'll see!" hollered Detective Jones over the roar of the helicopter.

As Jack's helicopter left English territory, the English police helicopter continued to pursue.

"Ohhhhh, shit!" exclaimed Jack. "They don't look like they care much about jurisdictional boundaries."

"No boundaries, I'd say! They shot at you for christ-sake! For what? A white-collar crime? And I thought these English bobbies didn't carry guns?"

"I don't think those were ordinary bobbies," explained Jack.

"Why not?" asked the detective.

"Well, they must send a special kind of police when money is stolen from a friend of the prince."

"Oh shit. I guess so. Which prince was it?"

"I didn't stick around to ask."

"Well," said the detective, "Once we're in France, I don't think they can make an arrest. I think they can only watch you and try to persuade the French authorities to arrest you."

"Do you know that for sure?"

"No."

"Keep going!"

Detective Jones kept flying as fast as the dual engine helicopter could go. As he approached a yacht, he began to descend.

"Hey, what are you doing?" asked Jack.

"I'm landing!"

"Where?"

"On Sarah's yacht. She has a helicopter pad."

"Sarah?" Jack asked bewildered.

"Cartwright!" Detective Jones clarified.

Jack laughed, both with relief and incredulity.

"You know," Detective Jones continued, "the former deputy D.A. from your office, who you thought had no right to leave her post serving justice, only to go and, I quote: 'live happily ever fucking after in the South of France.' "

Jack laughed even harder now. "Yeah, I remember. But boy am I sure glad she did!"

Jack then asked another question, "Are we already in the South of France?"

"No, this helicopter couldn't fly that far. Thankfully, Sarah was sailing near Normandy for book research this week. That's how I knew we had a safe landing pad in France, and flew straight here."

***

As Detective Jones carefully began his slow descent towards the yacht, Jack asked him a question: "How were you in the right place, at the right time, and in a helicopter!"

Detective Jones laughed, "When I found out who Venus really was, I figured you'd need a ride."

"But how were you there right at that moment?"

"Partly dumb luck, partly a call with Gil."

"Gil? How?"

"It's a long story."

"But How'd you get in a helicopter so fast?"

"I was already in it. I always like to use my pilot's license when I'm out here visiting Sarah. Sometimes I fly a plane, sometimes a helicopter. So I went to London and got into this double engine helicopter because I needed something that would go long distance. I had actually just gotten up into the air and wanted to practice landing it, when I got the call from Gil."

"Hold on. Did you say you wanted to practice landing it?"

"Yeah."

"You haven't landed this thing yet?"

"No. This is my first time."

"What the hell!"

"Relax. We'll be fine. That's why I'm taking my time here."

"I'll relax after we've landed!" Jack closed his eyes and prayed for dear life.

"Don't you want to hear the rest of it?" asked Detective Jones.

"After we've landed!" shouted Jack, with his eyes still closed.

***

Ten minutes later, the helicopter was safely on the helipad, and Detective Jones was shutting down the engine. It was not until after the engine became completely silent that Jack opened his eyes. When he did, he took a deep breath, inhaling a burst of fresh air.

Jack's heart was still pounding so hard, he could hear it thumping in his ears, almost as loud as the angry English police helicopter hovering overhead, shouting demands from a loud speaker.

Jack and Detective Jones exited the helicopter and hurried down the stairs to the third level of the yacht where Sarah Cartwright, and her husband, David Nolan greeted them.

Jack was received by a surreal scene of calm and elegance, which only confused his senses further.

Sarah had spread out a fabulous feast with lots of refreshing drinks at a luxurious table set for five people. A Frenchman, named Pierre sat in one seat at the table, beaming like an excited child. He was on the yacht enjoying the afternoon with Sarah and David, when Sarah got the call from Detective Jones to head out to sea where he could meet them to land on their helipad. Detective Jones had made the call while he was hovering over London trying to get Jack to look up and see him in the air. Pierre couldn't contain his excitement at such an enthralling story that could only originate in a place like Los Angeles, California, where movies were made. He was the first to suggest the second phase of Jack's escape route, after Sarah had hung up the phone with the detective, and David asked her: "Then, what do we do?"

Always the gracious hostess, Sarah had laid out the spread that now greeted Jack, as she believed he'd need fuel and rest before embarking on phase two, of his escape.

As Jack approached the table, confused by how calm the scene felt, despite a police helicopter buzzing overhead, demanding through a loud speaker that the yacht steer towards a nearby port, he spoke first to Sarah, thanking her profusely for being at the right place, at the right time.

Then Jack said, "I don't think I have time to enjoy this. I'm kind of on the run, you see."

Sarah and the others laughed at Jack's great sense of humor despite very stressful circumstances; and Detective Jones explained the plan to him:

"Actually Jack, we're going to wait them out." Pointing at the English police helicopter that circled above them, Detective Jones continued, "See, they are about to run low on gas, so they will have to turn back any minute now. Frankly, I'm surprised they've pushed it this far. It's starting to get dangerous for them, unless they think they can land here in France. More than likely, they will contact the French coast guard, and ask for their cooperation. We have to wait until that chopper disappears, before you can make your next move. We don't want them to see that you've left the boat. We will serve as the decoy and wait for the French coast guard to come to us. And when they do, I'll flash them this!" Detective Jones showed Jack his old badge from the Los Angeles Police Department.

Then Pierre piped in, "Yes! Then, you will come with me! If luck smiles on you today, we will take the dingy to shore, undetected.

"What then?" asked Jack.

"Pierre frowned and shrugged his shoulders with the nonsaluece that only a Frenchman could express while plotting an escape, "We do not know, yet," he explained. "Our first step was to rescue you from England."

"Will the French cooperate with the English in their manhunt of me?"

Pierre shrugged again, "Could be."

Jack stared at him, pressing for something more, anything more.

Pierre understood the question in Jack's eyes and answered simply: "We will just have to avoid the French police too!"

Jack looked up at the police helicopter circling overhead, shouting angry commands through its intercom at the passengers on Sarah's yacht, and he wondered how the hell he was ever going to get out of this. He then looked at Pierre who was now exchanging light hearted small talk and laughter with the others, and Jack realized that even if this small, happy, unworried Frenchman could get Jack to shore undetected, Jack's movements would still be limited. For how was Jack ever going to get back to the U.S. without his passport! It was still back at the hotel where he'd left three police officers knocked out cold.

CHAPTER 35

By coincidence, Venus' planned escape route of out London was strikingly similar to Jack's impromptu escape—only she now flew over the English Channel in a private plane, instead of a helicopter. Venus had slipped out of the hotel suite, unnoticed; and calmly exited the building, taking the elevator to the parking garage, where she started the stolen car that her brother had left there, with its new paint job and new license plates hiding it in plain sight. He parked the car there just before Venus had landed in England. He left the key to the stolen car in the top drawer of the night stand in the hotel suite adjoining the one Jack and Venus had shared. Under a false name, he is the one who booked that room into which Venus slipped after Jack's unfortunate encounter with the police. The car key was tucked inside the bible, at the beginning of the Corinthians passage. Once inside the vehicle, Venus calmly drove off, obeying all traffic laws as she drove the stolen car to where she boarded a charter jet. Her brother was already waiting there, after having received her text: "Fly." A text she'd sent just after hanging up the phone with Gil.

As they flew towards the English Channel, Venus looked back at the land they left behind, "I hate England."

"Me too," replied her brother.

"I'm glad we're never going back," she said.

"I won't miss it," agreed her brother, "After all, it is the place where mother and father died."

"And where their killers live."

"Now, Venus, I'm not sure you can say that."

"They're as much responsible as anything."

"They couldn't have known."

"If any one of them would've leant mother the money she needed, she never would've killed herself. And father would never have found her lifeless body, and killed himself with the same pills she took."

"Venus, that was a lifetime ago. You have to push those thoughts out of your mind. Dwelling on it will only cause you pain. We've stolen more money from the people who could've helped her, than our parents ever had, and much more than they ever could have borrowed to pay their debts. We've been living a very comfortable lifestyle off of those people you blame."

Venus responded with a sad murmur, "Yes, but without a mother or father."

Her brother had no words to console her. He just put his arm around her hoping to give her quiet comfort.

A few minutes later, her voice became stronger: "It still makes me angry. I read her suicide note a thousand times."

"Where? How?"

"Once I was old enough, I got ahold of the police records."

"Oh. I wish you hadn't. You didn't need to know the details."

"Why should you bear the burden alone? You tried to protect me for so long. It was kind of you to let me believe it was a car accident all those years, until I was old enough to understand."

Her brother nodded in silent acknowledgment.

Venus continued shedding her emotions as she tried to wash England out of her system, knowing now that she could never go back, "It's unbelievable, you know. Tiffany looked me right in the eye at that party I attended with Jack last night, and she didn't even know who I was."

"Tiffany?"

"Yes. The daughter of the Earl, remember her?"

"Your childhood friend who lived down the street from us?"

"Yes."

"She didn't recognize you?"

"Not in the slightest."

"But we were so young when we went to those orphanages that separated us and changed our names. We always knew no one from our past would ever recognize us."

"I know. That's why it was safe to start our business with them." Venus always referred to her career of larceny as a "business."

As the aircraft flew beyond the land and only the cold water of the English Channel lie beneath them, Venus continued to reflect on the past, "We knew their habits and their lifelong employees; but, they had no idea who we were."

"It was definitely a great start to an immensely successful career," her brother added, "And we have lived a life as luxurious and privileged as any of them enjoy. It's even better for us though, because we're free. We're all over the world, never putting on airs for anyone. Just enjoying the spoils of what we've earned. It's a shame we have to retire now."

Venus stared out the window into a dark blue abyss, "A damn shame," she agreed, as guilt rose within her, and she cursed herself for ever having been foolish enough to fall in love with Jack Wayne, the most senior prosecuting attorney in the Los Angeles County District Attorney's Office.

***

When the plane turned south towards Nice, France, the conversation changed to brighter and better things. There were four places in the world where Venus and her brother had never committed crimes. These places were held in reserve for their sanctuaries, in the event of a moment just like this one—the inevitable moment they would be required to suddenly cease all criminal activity and quietly disappear to safer lands, to retire from a life of crime and live off of what they had already tucked away safely in various offshore bank accounts, in Switzerland, Cyprus and other locations. The coded message: "It's time to send our favorite stallion out to pasture," was the alert one would give the other, depending on who first became aware of the danger of being caught. It was the phrase that would set their escape plan in motion. When Venus had made that phone call from Bel Air and said this very thing to her brother, he knew exactly what to do.

Venus' preferred sanctuary was Cyprus, an island so far East in the Mediterranean Sea that the next country over was Syria. Her brother's preferred sanctuary was a small island off the coast of Latin America. Each of them had clean, legally owned, retirement villas on a beach in each location, albeit purchased with stolen money, in cash. Although heavenly, these islands were about to become their prisons, because they now had to avoid travel to many places in the world, due to the fact that Venus' face was now known to both English and American authorities.

Their third sanctuary was Dubai, the only safe place they could store stolen property, which could be liquidated quickly and privately without raising suspicion. They were now heading to their fourth sanctuary, Monaco, which is one of very few places in the world that did not observe extradition to the United States of America. That is where they would change transportation before heading to their next destination, in case the English authorities had begun searching for Venus or seen her face on the surveillance cameras of the charter jet company who's jet they were currently traveling in. The private jet to Nice, combined with helicopter transportation to Monaco, had been previously booked on the account of one of Venus' many international 'clients' who frequently traveled between England and the French Riviera.

While still in Bel Air, Venus had instructed her pawn to tell the charter jet company to hold the plane in reserve for several days to enable the client of Venus' "client" to jump on at a last minute's notice, because the exact date it would be needed was not known, and that they only had an approximate time frame. The so called client of the "client" was a new alias Venus' brother created recently but had not yet used.

CHAPTER 36

The party of five tried to enjoy their meal as best they could with a noisy helicopter circling above, shouting commands that the boat dock immediately. They ignored the demands, and continued eating. Sarah was the first to bring up the question Jack had already asked Detective Jones on the helicopter.

"So, you have to tell us how this all came together. All I know is that Detective Jones called us with an urgent request and we met him where he asked us to. But how on earth, did things transpire from London?"

In response, Detective Jones repeated what he had told Jack in the helicopter. When he reached the point where he'd left off, he said:

"So, I'm in the air in London, I had just taken off, with two full tanks, thankfully, when I get this call from Gil. Together, we realize that Charlotte is Venus and she knows who Jack is. So I head straight for Jack's hotel hoping to find a safe place to land nearby and get him the hell out of there!"

Jack snickered and shook his head in disbelief, still in shock over the discovery of who Venus is.

Detective Jones continued, "Then just a few minutes later, I'm hovering over Jack's hotel, and I couldn't believe my eyes. A man who looked just like Jack was running down the fire escape, with officers waiting below. And just as I'm pulling in closer for a better look, I get another call from Gil! He's frantic. He's practically screaming. He says: 'She just called me! Charlotte just called me! The call came from an England number and all she said was: 'The police are chasing your friend near Harrods in London.' "

Sarah interrupted with a question: "Who's Charlotte?"

"That's the code name we used for the suspect we were pursuing, who is also the same woman who framed Jack. She framed him for the very crimes we were investigating her for," explained the detective.

"Amazing," said Sarah.

"So, as I was saying," continued the detective, "I'm in the air, and I hear that Jack is being chased by the English police, and I'm there, I'm flying overhead, and there's Jack! He has just jumped down from the fire escape, and he's surrounded!"

Pierre was overtaken with excitement, he exclaimed: "But how did Jack know to find you?"

"Well, it wasn't easy. I kept texting him and texting him, but as you can imagine, he was a little preoccupied. Finally, he looked up as I was nearing him with a rope dangling from the chopper. And good ole Jack! He jumped on! And the rest is history!"

Pierre clapped his hands as if pleased by the ending of a good movie. David and Sarah were equally awe struck by the harrowing story. But their good cheer was cut short when they saw the English police chopper begin to clear out.

"Time to go!" the detective instructed. And Jack jumped out of his seat ready for the next part of his escape.

CHAPTER 37

The sky was now growing dark with rain clouds, and the grey waters of the English Channel, along the French coastline looked bitter cold; but the good news was, the police helicopter had gone before Jack could see any sign of any boat that appeared to be operated by French authorities; though Pierre insisted, he could see one in the distance rushing towards them.

The trick was to get off of Sarah's yacht, before any authorities from any jurisdiction could see anyone leave the boat. Thankfully, Sarah's yacht had a plethora of options. Pierre's original plan to quietly take a dingy to shore was not Jack's first choice. Now fully immersed into the role of a common criminal, Jack had to start thinking like one. While waiting for the English helicopter to leave, he'd noticed a number of jet skiers going by. His best chances were to wait for another group of jet skiers to come by, at which point he and Pierre could hop onto Sarah's pair of jet skis dangling off her yacht, then mix in with the group of tourists, finding safety in numbers. The weather having grown poorer and poorer over the past 20 minutes, had sent most of the watersportsmen back to shore. So, Jack had only one chance left. It was the group of rowdy, screaming, wave jumping jet skiers headed towards them.

"They are too far away!" argued Pierre.

"It's our best chance," replied Jack.

"But that boat behind them, very close behind them, I swear to you, is a French police boat; and they are coming straight for us."

"How can you tell from here?"

"I know the colors."

"Well, if you can see it from here, then they'll see us leave this boat in that dingy, and I'll be caught for sure! They'll see the dingy leave the boat and our wake running directly from this yacht like a trail straight to our dingy.

"Won't they see the jet skis do the same thing?" asked Pierre.

"Not if we follow my plan."

Jack untied each jet ski and gave each one a shove with his foot so that it floated freely in the water. He then asked Pierre to tell the skipper to steer the yacht away from the jet skis and to turn the yacht so that it was directly facing the oncoming French police boat.

"Tell him to head towards it," Jack instructed.

"Head towards it!?" Pierre asked incredulously.

"Yes! That way they won't see us slip into the water from the back. And, the further the yacht gets away from the jet skis, the better it will be. Can you swim under water for a long distance?"

Pierre shrugged.

"You don't have to come with me, you know."

"Of course, I do!" Pierre insisted. "You don't know France! I must get you to my home in the South of France where you will be safe."

"How far is that from here?

"By boat, plane or car?"

Jack sighed and resigned himself to taking things one step at at time. "Nevermind, let's just get off this yacht undetected."

As the yacht headed towards the French police, and the jet skis floated away from it, Jack watched the wild group of seven jet skiers, and he calculated how long it would take them to near the jet skis that Jack had just freed from Sarah's yacht.

When Pierre hurried back down from his conversation with the skipper, he found Jack sitting at the back edge of the yacht.

"Listen, Pierre, we have to slip into the water without making a splash, then we have to swim as far as we can underwater. Don't pop your head up until we get to that group of seagulls sitting on the water about 20 feet from here, do you see those?"

"Yes, but birds in the water, sometimes mean sharks in the water," said Pierre.

"Let's assume they're dolphins not sharks."

"You can assume. I cannot assume"

"I can't do anything else, but assume, at this point."

"But those seagulls are not near the jet skis. They are to the left, deeper in the water, and the jet skis are to the right."

"Doesn't matter. We don't want any witnesses to see us leave the boat, or pop up out of the water too close to it. No matter how smooth Detective Jones will be when he flashes them his LAPD badge, I have a strong feeling the French police will be a little more loyal to their European counterparts than some American on a yacht with a badge they can't verify. So they'll be asking every boat in the water what they saw today."

"Yes, yes." Pierre agreed.

"That's why I asked him to turn the boat around and head towards them. He'll buy us time, but our only chance of really getting away is if we are not seen leaving the boat by anyone."

"Yes. I see." Pierre agreed again.

"That's why we'll slip in from this edge, because there are no boats on this side to see us slip into the water. As the yacht moves further away from us, we'll be swimming in the opposite direction, under water. When our heads pop out of the water in the middle of all those seagulls, it'll be hard for anyone to notice."

"Then what do we do?"

"Then we swim as fast as we can towards those jet skis. We'll have to get on and join that wild bunch as they pass by."

"They are being very careless, they're going to crash into something. Maybe even each other. They might crash into us!"

"I know. It's the perfect cover. We'll look like some of them fell off their jet skis, when we hop onto ours.

"Excellent idea!"

"And we'll have to ride as wild as they do, jumping their wakes, turning circles, hooting and hollering. We have to look like one of them."

"Perfect. But how do we get to shore?"

"After we become a part of their group for about 10 or 15 minutes, then we can break off and go our own way. It will look like we broke off from them. We'll dump the jet skis about 100 feet from shore, then swim in."

"I think we should take the dingy."

Jack laughed out loud, "That plan has long since passed, Pierre. We really can't take it now," Jack said, as he pointed at something in the near distance.

Pierre looked down the coastline and saw clearly what Jack was pointing at. Even Jack could see now the markings on the French police boat drawing ever closer to the yacht.

"Away we go!" Jack hollered, as he slipped into the water, and held his breathe, swimming below the surface as fast as he could.

Pierre quickly followed.

As Jack swam closer to the seagulls, he opened his eyes below the water and felt the sharp sting of salt water. He closed them quickly then reopened them, only more narrowed this time. He had to make sure he was swimming in the right direction.

It was hard to see with stinging eyes in murky waters. So he listened for the sound of the seagulls. They sounded nearer. That was good. But now, he could see a swarm of very large sea life directly in front of him. Large fins, large bodies, greyish colored skin. The words Pierre had spoken when they were still safe, dry and warm on the yacht, suddenly echoed in Jack's mind: "Birds in the water, sometimes mean sharks in the water." Heart racing fear gripped Jack and he almost panicked. He wanted to pop his head above water to clear his eyes so he could see what he was approaching. But it was too soon. The birds were still too far. He couldn't risk being seen. He hoped Pierre wouldn't panic either.

One of the large creatures began swimming towards Jack. He panicked, but stayed beneath the water. A quick sharp thought entered his mind. The answer to a trivia question. His friend the scuba diver knew it. What to do if a shark is too close to you underwater? Jack balled up his fist and pulled it back as far as he could, while still kicking hard to continue swimming forward, he aimed to punch the sea creature directly in the nose. That's what you do. You punch a shark in the nose to stun it into freezing. As it neared him, he swung his fist forward as hard as he could through the resistance of the water, punching as hard as possible. He missed. It swam passed him fast. So fast, the current moved his body backwards. A dolphin. Not a shark. Oh good, all of them were dolphins. Of course, it is dolphins that swim in pods.

Just as relief rushed over him, Jack reached the seagulls and popped his head out of the water for much needed air. He looked behind him. Pierre did the same thing. "You were right, Jack! They were dolphins!"

"Yes, they were!" Jack replied with excitement and relief.

After that scare, the jet skis seemed an easy target. They would get there in time. Jack and Pierre swam hard, each one reaching his jet ski just as the wild tourists came buzzing by on their own jet skis filling the area with waves and splashes and a chaotic watery scene. It was perfect.

Securely on each jet ski, Jack and Pierre revved each of theirs to maximum speed and blended right in with the tourists. They hooted and hollered and jumped the wakes of the other jet skis, spinning cookies in the water, and nearly falling in. But they stayed on. Jack let out a loud "Woo Hoo!" as the feeling of freedom coursed through his veins. It felt like he'd been holding his breathe since London. Now he could breathe. The speed of the jet ski made him finally feel in control. After 10 minutes, he waived at Pierre and pointed towards the coast. They sped towards it, just as the French police were boarding Sarah's yacht.

***

What Detective Jones had believed was going to be a reasonable conversation between law enforcement officers with a mutual respect for one another, was not. One French police officer accused him of getting his badge online. Another officer had heard of David Nolan and knew that he was in the movie business. Having recognized his name when David gave it to him, he then accused David of giving Detective Jones a movie prop to try and fool the French authorities.

Knowing things were going south, quickly, Sarah ran around the yacht locking doors and demanding that the police could not open that door, or walk down that staircase or turn down that corner. It was a ploy to get them to believe that Jack was still on the boat, so she could buy him more time to get further and further away. It was a very large yacht, and she could keep up the charade for at least an hour, maybe two if she created enough chaos by screaming, "No! not there, please don't look there!" She would play the quintessentially hysterical female. First pretending to give in to their demands, promising to let them into another locked room, if they just don't make a mess of things, then refusing to do so, then fumbling with 15 different keys to unlock doors.

Finally, growing ever more frustrated with Sarah's shenanigans, the officers threatened to arrest her. So, she gave them a set of unmarked keys and wished them good luck. They were the keys to her house in Malibu, not her yacht in France.

On the yacht's deck, Detective Jones continued arguing with another French police officer.

"He's not a fugitive!" screamed Detective Jones.

"He is, sir," insisted the French officer.

"No! He is a law enforcement officer, just as you and I are."

"You are not a police officer. Not here. Maybe in the movies in Hollywood, but not here!"

"Call LAPD! Call the LA District Attorney's Office, you can verify this so easily. Just do it!"

"I do not take instructions from you. I take instructions from my senior officer. Nobody on this boat leaves. You are all under arrest for assisting a fugitive."

"You can't even prove he was here," Sarah said calmly as she walked down the stairs to the deck where Detective Jones argued with the French officer.

"We are searching this yacht, madam. And nobody can leave until we are through."

"Make yourselves comfortable," Sarah replied, "Would you like a cocktail?"

"Don't be ridiculous!" shouted the police officer, "This is not a game. And if we don't find your friend on this yacht, we will catch him wherever he goes. We have secured every airport in France. He will not get away."

It would be several hours before the French police would leave Sarah's yacht. In the meantime, Sarah and Detective Jones made their calls to L.A. trying to arrange talks between law enforcement officers there and in France.

The French refused to yield their investigation. They insisted that the suspect must first be captured and then the talks could be begin.

Detective Jones tried for diplomacy again. He thought maybe he could mix a little diplomacy with peer pressure to see if he could get some cooperation with the officers searching Sarah's yacht.

"So, why are you so eager to help the English with one of their cases, even if the English botched that case by letting the real criminal slip away right under their noses—only to start chasing an American law enforcement officer who is investigating that very same suspect?"

"Sir! This! is a matter for the French, not the English!"

"What do you mean?"

"One cannot steal from a Duke of France and expect to be released with a few phone calls from Hollywood!"

"Ooooh shiiiit.... Not you guys too," Detective Jones gave up any hope of negotiating Jack's amicable release to L.A. authorities.

CHAPTER 38

Wet, sandy and exhausted, Jack and Pierre walked with heavy legs up the beach in silence, each one of them scanning the coast for any sign of police officers searching for them. So far, it looked like they were safe.

"So, what now?" Jack asked. "What is the fastest way to get to your house in the South of France?"

"By plane," answered Pierre.

"I can't board a plane. My passport and all other identification is still in London."

"You do not need it. We will fly on my private plane."

Jack's eye brows shot up in surprise. "You just happen to have a private plane waiting for us?"

"Not just happen to. I flew here in it, to meet Sarah and David. I am not crazy like them to spend weeks on a boat, sailing all the way here from the South of France. You have to go all the way around to get all the way up here. They have been sailing for weeks. They planned their sailing route, based on their plans to meet Detective Jones in Normandy, a few days from now. But he dropped in early, with you! I never expected this much excitement! I'm glad I agreed to meet them on their boat once they got to the English Channel."

"So, how far is your plane?"

"Not too far by taxi. My money is wet, but it is still in my pocket. I can get us a taxi to where my plane is. My pilot is always near the plane."

Jack counted his blessings and considered himself lucky that Sarah's new lifestyle included her own yacht, and friends with airplanes. He now laughed at himself for previously mocking the lifestyle, long ago, when Detective Jones first informed Jack that Sarah had flown off into the sunset with a Hollywood filmmaker to go live in the lap of luxury in South of France; and that she had no plans to come back to work at the District Attorney's Office. Jack now gratefully conceded, this was a lifestyle that could sure come in handy sometimes. He wondered if one more lucky break might bless him today.

"Any chance your private plane could fly me all the way to L.A.?" Jack asked Pierre.

"Ah, mon amie, I wish it could. But I only have a small plane. It can only fly within France. I do not leave France. Normally, I do not even leave my house. It has been a very long time since I left my own house. David and Sarah are the only ones I come out for anymore. They convince me to join them here and there, sometimes."

"How do you know Sarah and David?"

"I met them over a mutual love: Art!" Pierre emphasized and pronounced the word "art" as if speaking a sacred word. After holding the word in the air with his emotions, in a brief pause, he continued answering Jack, "David and Sarah are my very good friends. They come to visit a painting inside my house every week, and we have long, interesting conversations over wine, cappuccino, or champagne, depending on how we feel that day."

Jack shook his head at the image of the stellar prosecutor he once knew, now sipping champagne in France and talking about nothing with this funny little Frenchman, while she "visited" a painting at his house. Jack tried not to laugh out loud. His image of Sarah had always been of a winning Deputy District Attorney who showed no mercy for the guilty. Her talent in the courtroom rivaled even the undefeated, Sam Chapman. She was a legend. Jack wondered how Sarah could give up such an admirable career. During these past six months that Jack had been playing the part of a Bel Air billionaire, he found himself getting very bored, often. He didn't understand Sarah's choice; but, he was very glad she made it.

The Frenchman interrupted Jack's thoughts with a sudden announcement regarding the next leg of their journey. "We will fly to Nice!" he declared. "That is where I flew from. My sports car is still parked there. So, we will fly back there, and drive to my home not very far away from there."

CHAPTER 39

Venus' flight from London to Nice, France was a comfortable one. She and her brother used the two hour flight to change their appearance. Venus now wore a short blonde wig, cut in the style of a bob. In London, she had been seen with her natural, long dark hair. The hairstyle she wore for Jack, because she had wanted him to know her natural self. Now, she chose the exact opposite look. It was necessary, in case she too may have ended up on the radar of the French or English authorities. She also changed her clothes, her shoes, and her handbag. Her brother was more careful. He used prosthetics to change the appearance of his face. A larger nose, a pointier chin, hairier eyebrows. He didn't need a wig, he just shaved his head, sporting the bald look. A wardrobe change was also necessary. He and Venus both dressed in the comfortable but fashionable clothes of wealthy tourists.

First, they would land where the private jets land at the Nice airport. From there, they would take a helicopter to Monaco, which does not observe extradition to the United States. Then, they would take a yacht to Venus' destination, Cyprus. They would sail the Mediterranean Sea from Monaco, where they had access to a yacht moored at Port Hercule. It was registered in the name of a Middle Eastern prince who had purchased it from them in Dubai, but still had not taken possession of it. In fact, he did not even know that it was already registered in his name. He thought it was still registered to its previous owner, which was nothing but another shell company Venus had set up in an offshore, untraceable entity.

Upon landing in Nice, Venus and Victor encountered delays. The helicopter they had reserved for travel to Monaco was not available, due to maintenance issues. However, they were in a hurry. They would not truly be safe until they were on that yacht in Monaco. Victor paced up and down the rows of helicopters, looking for an alternative. He bargained with each pilot who adamantly refused to bump their scheduled passengers. He even tried bribery, but so far no takers. Venus became anxious and walked towards the row of sports cars parked not very far away. Some were available for rent, while others were privately owned, and awaited their owners return. She paced up and down looking for one she could start without the key, while Victor continued to bargain with various helicopter pilots awaiting their passengers. Victor was also a pilot. All he needed to do was to convince one of them that he worked for the same charter company, and to let him take the helicopter and leave it with another pilot in Monaco to return.

45 minutes later he found a taker. Now, he just had to find Venus. He didn't see her sitting inside the sports car that she kept running idle, just in case.

***

After landing in Nice, Jack and Pierre hurried off of the plane and sprinted towards the sports cars. Jack stayed one step behind Pierre who knew which car he was looking for. When they reached his vehicle, Jack stopped to catch his breathe while Pierre fumbled around in search of his keys.

Though he didn't quite believe it, Jack heard a familiar voice in the distance.

"Over here, Victor," is what he heard her say. The voice rang in his ears like shot gun fire.

"Where?" Jack heard a man call out.

"Here. I'll come to you now," Jack heard the woman's voice again. He turned towards the sound.

It was unmistakably her. He watched her stand as she exited the vehicle, and when she did, her eyes met his. Striking blue eyes, startled blue eyes. Caught like a deer in the headlights Venus froze, her wide eyes meeting Jack's heated glare.

Rage coursed through Jack's veins as his eyes locked in on Venus' face. Forgetting momentarily that he was a suspect on the run, Jack reverted to his true crime-fighting self. He pointed at Venus and hollered: "Stop her!"

Unfortunately for Jack, in that exact same moment, the French police pointed at Jack and hollered, "Stop him!"

As Venus fled, running towards her brother, Jack sprinted after her, and the French police sprinted after Jack.

The helicopters were a distance away, and Venus had run so fast, she was almost there. Jack had to run zig zag through parked cars before he could reach an open space to gain enough speed to catch her. The French police did the same thing, chasing Jack.

Pierre watched in horror, but he was quick in his thinking. He fired up his engine and peeled out of his parking spot, speeding straight for the open space Jack was headed for. A scarf and fedora still in his passenger seat from before, Pierre wrapped the scarf around his face with one hand, while driving madly with the other. He pulled the oversized fedora down further to mask his identity. He swerved, almost hitting a parked car. He regained control, cruising towards the open space Jack was running for.

As Pierre cruised through it, Venus and Victor ran in front of Pierre's car and he slammed his brakes, coming to a screeching halt, separating Jack from Venus and Victor. Jack cussed out loud, and Pierre jumped out of the car and shoved Jack inside.

A French police car was already behind him, and the ones on foot pursuing Jack almost caught Pierre before he slammed the door shut and peeled out again.

As Victor and Venus entered their aircraft and took off, Pierre raced down the road at break neck speed.

Jack cussed and turned in his seat, watching Venus get away.

"Put your seat belt on Jack! These are dangerous roads!" Pierre yelled as he came screeching around a corner. The windy roads forced Pierre to slow his speed, and the French police car was hot on his tail. He wound around the mountains wildly, straddling the center line with his car, straight into on-coming traffic. Pierre swerved back into his lane at the last second to avoid one head on collision, then almost another and another.

"Christ almighty!" Jack screamed.

"It will force the police to slow down," Pierre explained as he continued his mad and wild ride winding up the hills higher and higher.

Jack looked out his window down the side of a steep cliff and swore again.

The French police were relentless, chasing Pierre's car with just as much madness as Pierre drove it.

***

Up high in the sky were Venus and Victor watching the whole thing from their helicopter.

"Venus, you are out of your mind!" her brother argued. "I can't keep following them. What do you expect me to do?"

"I don't know, just keep flying low, like a tourist's helicopter. I want to see what happens to Jack."

Unable to resist his sister's wishes, Victor gave in and continued following the car chase.

***

As Pierre kept winding up the traitorous hills of the South of France, higher and higher, the cliffside became steeper and steeper, and the French police car grew closer and closer.

Finally, Pierre slammed on his brakes, and the car fishtailed almost to the edge of the cliff before he regained control, and forced the car into the embankment. This caused the French police to slam on their brakes and suffer almost the same fate. But they missed Pierre's car by a hair.

Their bodies jerked forwards and backwards hard, and when the police regained their composure they watched the suspects flee the vehicle, on foot, running up a steep mountainside into nowhere. They followed.

Jack ran up the hill behind Pierre into thick brush and trees. There was no trail. Pierre blazed his own trail.

The police were unshakeable. They followed.

***

Still hovering above the chase was the helicopter carrying Venus and Victor.

"Can we save him?" Venus asked.

"No! Of course not!"

"Why not?"

"Did you forget he was chasing you?"

"No."

"Well?"

"When he sees the evidence against him, he'll have to retire with me."

"Venus, you are out of your mind. That is a cop! He is a police officer!"

"No. He is a lawyer."

"A prosecuting attorney," Victor emphasized, "That's the leader of the police officers!"

"But he needs to escape, too. He'll be safe in Cyprus, with me."

Having heard enough of his sister's delusions, Victor pulled on a lever, and the helicopter rose high into the sky. "Get him out of your sight and out of your mind, Venus. He will be your downfall. And there is no way we could ever land and board him in time. Those cops are right on his tail. And there is nothing but a solid mountain at the end of his path. Venus, your lover boy is going to be caught for sure. And that's just how we planned it. Now move on."

"But I didn't think he'd fight. I thought he'd go easily in London."

"So?"

"So, that means he's like us. It means he'll be happy with me, on the run."

"No. It doesn't it."

As Victor pulled the helicopter up and headed towards Monaco, Venus twisted in her seat desperately, looking back to watch for as long as she could, what would come of Jack.

The last thing she saw made her cry and sob out loud.

***

As Pierre and Jack climbed higher up the hill, Jack couldn't see an end in sight to the wild brush and trees. The hill kept getting steeper. They could still hear the police behind them shouting, and they were still within view of the officers, until they rounded the mountain.

Suddenly, Pierre stopped and grabbed Jack to duck between trees. Jack's foot slipped and he almost slid clear down a one hundred foot cliff.

"Not yet, Jack," Pierre hollered as if Jack meant to do so.

Pierre then started peeling off layers of clothing—his fedora, his scarf, his windbreaker, his shoes. And, one at a time, he threw each one down the side of the cliff 50 feet in the opposite direction.

"Now yours!" he instructed Jack.

Bewildered, Jack handed him his jacket.

"And your shoes!" Pierre demanded.

One at a time, Pierre threw Jack's shoes down the hill, making it appear as if someone had tumbled down and lost their clothing. He tore the jacket against a branch about 50 feet away from where Jack stood, partially breaking the branch, which hung over the edge of the cliff. He left part of the torn jacket on the remaining portion of the branch, and threw the other part down the hill.

In French, Pierre could hear one officer yell, "There, I see their footprints going that way!"

The officers were too close.

Pierre turned and ran back to where Jack stood. When he got there, he said, "Now!"

"Now, what?"

"Now jump!"

"Off the cliff?!"

"Aim for those bushes," Pierre pointed to the spot where Jack almost fell into, earlier. Bushes jetted out from the side of the cliff, about six feet below, but all around those bushes was nothing but air.

"Those bushes won't hold me!"

"They're not supposed to."

Pierre heard one officer holler in French, "They turned through these trees! Follow me!"

There was no time. Pierre shoved Jack over the cliff. Jack fell backwards, screaming the blood curling scream of a man falling to his death.

CHAPTER 40

Inside the Los Angeles District Attorney's Office, Sam Chapman walked quickly down the hallway and barged into the private office of the District Attorney. Sam blurted out the reason for his visit, without even the courtesy of a greeting.

"I guess you won't be retiring this year, after all," Sam pestered the D.A.

"The hell I won't be!" the D.A. barked.

Sam quickly retorted, "Jack was your heir apparent. Who is going to run in your place, now?"

"Jack will!"

"A little difficult after I just saw him on the news, dangling from a rope outside of a helicopter, with foreign cops shooting at him."

"What!"

"Yeah, it's a big story. The English public are demanding to know why their own police officers are shooting at people in their streets the way a bunch of wild, violent American police officers might do."

"Sam, what the hell are you talking about!"

Sam clicked the remote control and turned on a foreign news channel. They both watched as the anchor man described the video on the screen, which depicted two helicopters in the sky above London, with one man dangling by a rope outside one of the helicopters. The news man spoke as the video played. He described the explanation given by officials for the wild display in the streets of London: "Officials say that bystanders mistook the filming of a fictional movie for real events." The news then flashed to a clip of bystanders being interviewed, all of whom adamantly denied seeing any cameras or movie crews anywhere near the area. That clip was quickly followed by an official explaining that the camera crew was inside the second helicopter that was hovering in the sky next to the police helicopter.

Sam then turned off the T.V. and said, "Well, so far, I guess Jack's name is safe from the media. It looks like the English authorities have a bigger secret to keep than we do."

"What secret, Sam!"

"Sorry, I guess I better fill you in. Jack Wayne was framed by the suspect he's been investigating for running a crime ring in L.A. Only, her crime ring is not limited to L.A. It's international. So she lured him to London to frame him for her own crimes there. Pretty brilliant, isn't she? She lured him outside his jurisdiction, where he'd have no power, and she left him a sitting duck to take her fall. Luckily, Detective Jones was in the vicinity. That's who was really flying that other helicopter. He got Jack out of there in the nick of time. Now Jack's somewhere in Europe without his passport. We don't know where he is because he doesn't have his cell phone either. The last Detective Jones saw of him, he was slipping into the water off a yacht near Normandy, France. Jack has gone into hiding until we can clear his name."

Staring at Sam in disbelief for several long seconds of silence, the District Attorney then turned his head to look at his calendar. He felt utterly dismayed by the fact that today was not April Fool's Day.

CHAPTER 41

The bone chilling sound of a man falling to his death caused the French police officers to freeze in place. They stood silent for a few long seconds, staring at each other. Then slowly, they tiptoed passed the trees where the footsteps led. The first thing that caught their eye was Jack's torn jacket on a branch 50 feet in the opposite direction from where Pierre had shoved him down the cliff.

At first glance, the footsteps led directly to that broken branch that held Jack's torn jacket, dangling in the wind. The sound they had just heard, and the sight of the torn jacket told them everything they needed to know. Most of the officers stood in place at the break in the trees where Jack and Pierre had first entered the area. The edge of the cliff was far too near for any more of them to step further in.

One brave officer tiptoed towards the broken branch, and very carefully peered over the hill. Tangled in the branches below were the clothing of two men, not just one. He shook his head, said a quick prayer for the departed, and walked back to his fellow officers.

The French officers left the scene without ever looking in the other direction, where Pierre had shoved Jack down the cliff. However, even if they had, they would not have been able to detect what occurred.

The shrubs that Jack fell into were six feet down a 90 degree cliff. Too far down for anyone to inspect. After Jack fell through them, they bounced back up. To an onlooker, the shrubs would not look any different than wild dangling shrubs of any untamed cliff. Even if they had walked over to inspect the area, the French officers would not have known that, immediately after Jack was shoved off the cliff, Pierre intentionally jumped into the exact same spot.

When the shrubs bounced back up, after each man fell through them, the shrubs covered what lie beneath: a trap door, leading to a tunnel.

Jack went sliding down first, and landed on hard dirt. Before he could even collect his bearings, Pierre came sliding down and crashed right into him.

Glad to be alive, but cussing from the pain, Jack finally said, "What the hell is going on here!"

Pierre explained. "I could not drive you to my house with the police on our trail. So I had to fake that crash into the hill so we could come running up this way to enter through the tunnel."

"What is this place?"

"This is a very important place. It is filled with important history, and love, and was once filled with the best treasures of the world."

"How long will we be hiding here."

"We will not stay here. We will walk through the tunnel."

"What if they come after us?"

"They cannot see the tunnel. I jumped before they passed the trees. Nobody saw me, and the shrubs will cover the trap door. The cliff looks too dangerous for anyone to inspect. If it worked to keep the Nazis out. It will certainly keep those police officers out."

"Nazis?"

"Yes. This tunnel was built by my great grandfather and his friends in the French underground, during WWII. They used it to hide the artwork they stole back from the Nazis who stole it out of our fine museums."

"Wow," Jack looked around, but couldn't see anything but darkness."

Pierre, continued his history lesson, "The paintings were hidden here until it was safe to put them back in the Louvre and the other museums."

"So, where will this tunnel take us?"

"To my house. It is five miles this way."

"Five miles!"

"Yes. In order to keep the paintings safe, the entrance had to be a great distance from the house so that they could never be discovered. That is how I thought of it today. I knew I could not drive the police straight to my house. So I went the opposite direction, knowing I could take this tunnel, if we were able to outrun them. And we did!"

"That was quick thinking. I'm sure glad I didn't talk you out of coming with me when we were on Sarah's yacht!"

"I am glad too, mon amie!"

As Jack and Pierre hiked the five mile walk underground to Pierre's house, Pierre continued his tour guide's talk of the tunnel and what it means to him and his family.

"Because of you, mon amie, I was able to experience the thrill of the stories my great grandfather used to tell me about this tunnel. He told me a million stories, and I always imagined what it would be like. How the trap door worked, What it felt like it? What if you missed it when you jumped off the cliff?"

"You mean, we might have missed the trap door?"

"Of course!"

"And you shoved me, anyway?!"

"There was no other way! You would have been caught!"

"Oh, geez....." Jack shook his head, and counted his blessing again for the hundredth time that day.

Then another thought came to him, "Wait, are you telling me, you've never used this tunnel before?"

"Of course not. Nobody has used it since World War II."

"Then how did you know it still worked?"

"I didn't."

"So, we could've been killed or caught?"

"Probably only caught. If the door did not work, then we only would have landed on hard metal, under the shrubs."

"And how would we have climbed back up that six feet of cliff?"

"That, would have been difficult."

"Any other difficulties you want to warn me about, that I might encounter over these next five miles?"

"No."

"Are you sure? I've had a few too many surprises today."

"Well...."

"Well, what?"

"I do not know if we can get the exit door open. It is sealed under the tile floor of my gallery."

Jack took a deep breath and prayed for good fortune.

CHAPTER 42

While Jack was walking in the dark down a five mile tunnel, with no end in sight, and still wondering if there was even a way out of the tunnel, the District Attorney's Office in Los Angeles was working hard to clear his name.

They would be forced to work with the English authorities first. Strangely, the French authorities were silent. They would not state whether or not they had captured Jack Wayne; and they were not asking or answering any questions, either. They insisted that the Americans should first work through the English, and after the English advised them whether Jack Wayne was guilty or innocent, then they would provide information about Jack Wayne's whereabouts, to the extent possible.

"To the extent possible? What the hell does that mean!" Sam Chapman asked the District Attorney.

The District Attorney turned up his palms in question, "That's all they would say."

"Well is he, or isn't he in their custody?"

"They wouldn't say."

"What kind of bullshit is that?"

"French bullshit, I guess."

"Well, aren't they concerned about the money of their Duke? Why should we cooperate with them, if they won't even tell us where Jack is?"

"Thanks to your quick action, and that of Gil Ramirez, every penny of stolen money is frozen. They figure their Duke's money is safe there, and that he will get his money back, once we and the English resolve the case, and agree to release funds back to their rightful owners."

"That could take weeks!" Sam exclaimed.

"You're right. Given the way this woman who framed Jack operates, we will have to be very careful in our due diligence to ensure that each incoming wire came from a legitimate owner. That could take some time."

Sam replied, "And, in the meantime, we all have no idea where Jack is?!"

"That sums it up."

"Why the delay? It doesn't give the French any leverage to delay telling us what happened to Jack."

"They said they have to first identify the second individual who drove the get away car before they can release any information about either of them."

"Get away car?"

"Yes, from the Nice airport, a sports car was stolen—at least they assume it was stolen, because there is no connection between the owner of the vehicle and Jack. Also, another car in the same parking lot was found running idle, after it had been hot wired. So, they assume Jack and the getaway driver were planning on stealing two cars, but were interrupted when the police arrived, so they both jumped into one car. That's where Jack was last seen. Somebody else was driving. They couldn't see the driver's face because he was wearing an oversized fedora which was pulled down low, covering most of his face."

"So ... what? Do they think, we know who the getaway driver is?" asked Sam.

"No. They have to withhold the information until they can identify next of kin."

"Next of kin? That means they think he's dead!"

"The driver not Jack."

"We don't even know that for sure."

"No. We don't. All we can do now is focus on what we can control. Sarah Cartwright and Detective Jones are in France. We'll work with them in trying to locate Jack."

"But they were on the yacht he landed on when escaping the English authorities. If he's in hiding, we don't want Sarah and Detective Jones to lead the authorities to Jack, until we've cleared him."

"But if he's in trouble, we need to find him fast."

"Agreed."

"We also need to work fast towards his exoneration. The French said they will follow the English on this. I'm scheduling calls with the English authorities, as soon as possible.."

"Good. And I'll make sure we fast track all the cases against Charlotte's pawns. Or Venus, or whoever the hell she is."

***

The District Attorney's personal office was the largest in the Los Angeles County D.A.'s Office. It was a corner office the size of one of their mid-sized conference rooms, and it was decorated with the warmth of a traditional law office. A cherry wood desk and matching shelves, storing lots of law books were complimented by dark brown leather chairs. Two oversized and comfortable arm chairs sat across his desk, where he could confer with his top prosecutors and other important people.

Today, he was not seated at his desk. Instead, he was seated at the opposite end of the room where more brown leather arm chairs circled a coffee table. This area was meant for long, involved meetings—the kind that would require the D.A. to settle in a place more comfortable than his office chair, but still stiff and professional enough to keep him focused. He sat in the chair that faced out the window. This is where he sat whenever he needed to speak to someone in a call that would require him to be on his toes, and in perfect form. It is where he sat when talking to the press about sensitive issues. It is where he had sat on many occasions with his campaign manager before each election he had won over the past 20 years. Today, the phone call he was on was far more important than that.

The District Attorney had started the call with the English police on a positive note, while calmly seated in his chair. He had explained to them that Jack had been a loyal and trusted employee of the District Attorneys' Office for over 20 years, and that a long line of reputable police officers, judges and prosecutors could vouch for his credibility. He further explained that Jack was working undercover at the time he was in England, and that they were badly mistaken about who the real suspect was.

However, the English police were stubborn and refused to call off their investigation of Jack Wayne. Instead, they insisted that the District Attorney had a duty to turn Jack over to them (suggesting, his office was helping Jack evade European authorities). They also explained that they were putting pressure on the French to continue their manhunt, despite the strange nonchalance the French had suddenly begun to exhibit.

One hour into the call, the District Attorney was now standing, and hollering:

"The real suspect is the woman who was in the very room your officers barged into when they tried to arrest my colleague! She was right under your noses, within reach. Right there in front of you, and you let her go!"

The English police officer scoffed in response, "The only person whose name was on the bank account that received the fraudulent wire transfers was: Jack Wayne. He had no accomplices," the officer insisted.

The District Attorney retorted: "Well, if he's the only one on the account, he has complete authority to reverse the wires, in which case there is no theft, and no case."

The English officer responded: "We are not Americans, we don't let people buy their freedom."

"How dare you!"

"I do dare!"

"That's not how we do things here, and that's not even what I'm suggesting."

"Oh no? What about that case you had, right there in your city, L.A., a few years ago? Why did that movie producer who killed the actress go free? And before that, why did that famous football player who killed his ex-wife go free? We watch your news. We see how you do things there."

"What the hell are you talking about! They both stood trial! They didn't pay to go free! In each case, a jury found them not guilty."

"Your country does that a lot for rich people."

"Hey! Nobody here is talking about buying freedom! My colleague is innocent! And you have no real evidence to convict him. Please don't remind me why the American revolution was necessary. I know if it were up to you, you'd torture a confession out of him, and throw him in jail without a trial."

"Oh stop that!"

"You stop your nonsense. I am the District Attorney of Los Angeles County. You are talking about my most senior deputy, who has been a long-time employee of this office and who has impeccable integrity, and a stellar reputation. And I am flat out telling you the only reason he was in your country was because he was undercover investigating a white collar criminal who engages in the same activity of which you accuse him. Any idiot can see she framed him for her own crimes to get him off her tail."

"Did you just call me an idiot?"

"Yes."

"Well that does it! I'm hanging up. If you won't cooperate, we have other means. We'll seek extradition."

"From where? France?"

"The French don't have him. They've ended their manhunt, so he must be in your country by now."

The District Attorney gulped hard at the news that the French ended their manhunt. He didn't know if that was good news or bad. It was an unnerving and distracting news flash from the unknowing Englishman; but the D.A. couldn't allow himself to be distracted with such thoughts at this moment. Right now, he had to get this call under control.

"Now hold on," he said. "Just hold on a minute," The D.A. said, trying to calm things down, "I didn't mean any offense. I apologize. Just bear with me a moment. Let me talk you through this."

"Fine. Please continue."

"Ok, hear me out. This is a property crime. If the property is returned to its owner it's not stolen."

"I told you before, we . .. "

"Just a minute. What evidence do you have that Jack Wayne initiated the wire from the victim's account to the account you say bears his name?"

A long silence followed.

"Well," nudged the D.A., "Do you have an answer?"

"We don't know who initiated the wire. We only know where the money ended up."

"That's not enough to prove Jack did it."

"He benefitted from it. That's enough for us to convict him."

"Not if you can't even prove that he was even aware the account existed."

"We have his signature on documents opening the account."

"How could you possibly know what his signature looks like?" pressed the District Attorney.

"We compared it to his passport signature. It looks the same."

"Is that all you can say? It looks the same?"

"We will get an expert. He will say that, although not identical, the signatures were made by the same person."

"Not identical?" taunted the D.A., "Not identical? What does that mean?"

"Only a bit sloppy, not different. Perhaps, he was drunk when he signed the bank signature card."

"And how will you present that case theory without a blood draw?"

Silence followed the D.A.'s question, so he pressed the English officer further.

The taunting tone still in his voice, the D.A. asked, "I suppose you will also produce video from the bank's surveillance camera showing Jack Wayne's face at the bank signing those documents?" The D.A. asked the question, gambling on the assumption that it was impossible for the English police to produce such evidence.

The English police officer stumbled over his words in response, "Well, um, you see . . . uh, we can't do that."

"Why not?" persisted the D.A.

"We just cannot do so."

"Because it doesn't exist!" shouted the D.A., "You know damn well Jack never walked into any English bank and he never signed any goddamned documents!"

"There is no reason to get vulgar, sir."

"Of course there is! You want the blood of an innocent man because you have failed miserably at catching the real criminal."

"That is not what we want, sir!"

"How about this? Do you want the press to know how incompetent your banks are at protecting people's money? You can't identify who initiated the wires from the victim's accounts. You can't identify who, how, where or when, the documents opening the receiving account were signed. You have told me that one of the victims is a very close friend of the prince. Now, please tell me this, if you can't protect people who are that important to your country, then what good are you?"

Dead silence met the D.A.'s harsh questions. The D.A. continued.

"And, what about that shooting incident in the streets of London? I have a witness who will testify, that was no movie scene."

"That wasn't our police!" the English officer protested.

"Then who was it!"

"It was the private security of the victim. He's been admonished already."

"Well, I guess I'll just tell the press you told them only a little white lie, then?"

"No!"

"I guaranty you one thing. If you do not close this case, with a conclusion that Jack Wayne is innocent of all suspicion, I will personally call every press outlet in your country and reveal these facts."

"That will not be necessary, sir."

"So," concluded the D.A., "When can I expect a written report confirming that you have closed the case against Jack Wayne, which expressly states that, in your opinion, he is a victim too, and is innocent of all suspicion?"

"That will take some time."

"I sure hope you get around to it before I start calling your press tomorrow."

"No!!!" shouted the English police officer, nervously.

"Then, I'll ask you again. When can I expect that succinct report?"

"We need to see the evidence first. You must cooperate with us."

"Of course, we'll cooperate. Just tell me what you need from us."

"We need your evidence in the case you say Jack Wayne was investigating."

"Fine. You'll get it."

CHAPTER 43

Jack and Pierre finally made it to the end of the long dark tunnel. Their eyes had adjusted to the dark by now. Also, the matches in Pierre's pocket had finally dried, so they were able to light a stick they found to serve as a torch.

Unlike the front of the tunnel, which was high and curved, to serve as a slide forcing the entrant down and inward towards the hillside where the tunnel continued, this end of the tunnel was shorter. The height of the tunnel at it's end, was barely above Jack's head. This made it easy for him to inspect the exit door, which was overhead. It too was made of metal. But it was unlike the entering trap door, which had two slabs of metal intertwined with a series of connecting 'v" shaped ends that opened as soon as weight hit the top, dropping the weight into the tunnel, then springing back up to close as soon as the weight had dropped, thereby resuming its appearance as the shrubbery, with which the top side of the metal was covered.

The exit door had only one slab of metal and a handle that Jack could reach by lifting his arm up. It was presumably placed there to allow tunnel occupants to pull down on it, in order to open the door.

Jack could not see a lock, and the seems looked sealed tight. In the dark, he couldn't tell if the seems were cement or just old dirt. He inspected the seams carefully before trying to pull down on the handle.

"Pierre," he called out, "Do you know what was used to seal the door shut?"

"It is not the door that is sealed. It is my floor above it. One large heavy piece of tile covers the door. Just like any tile floor, it is sealed to the other tiles."

"Oh, that's good news," said Jack. "Here, hold the torch while I try to pull the door open."

Jack tugged on the door as hard as he could, but nothing happened. Dirt fell from all around, showering Jack and Pierre.

Now dusting themselves off and spitting out dirt, the pair agreed to try something else.

"Let's see if we can find any rocks, Pierre," suggested Jack. "Try to find pointy ones. We'll use them as our tools."

The two hunted around in the dark, with one makeshift torch between them and they looked for rocks. Jack found one that fit well inside the grip of his right hand. It was narrow with an oval rounded edge. But it wasn't sharp.

"What did you find, Pierre?"

"Nothing. All fat round rocks."

Pierre held out a rock and Jack took it from him. He began scraping the rock in his hand against it, trying to chisel it to a point.

"Excellent!" said Pierre, "We'll make our own tools!"

Tired, and still wet from the first part of his escape, Jack was sick of being stuck in a damp, dark tunnel. He chiseled his rock with determination, swinging fast, as he hit one rock against the other, with hard, fast repetition. He was determined to create the tool he needed to unseal the door. First, he chiseled one side of his rock, then he flipped it over and chiseled the other. Finally, 40 minutes later, he had what he needed. Jack pushed the tip of the sharpened rock into the seem of the metal door, where the metal met the dirt between the edge of the door, and the surrounding tunnel. He scraped away hardened dirt all along the entire edge of the door, until it looked like he could see another material behind what he had scraped away.

Upon completion, he placed his rock on the ground, took a deep breath, and said a little prayer. He then grabbed the long handle with both hands, and yanked it down as hard as he could.

It came down, and almost knocked Jack to the ground. He ducked out of its way, and sat down on the ground, letting the door swing on its hinge. Pierre cheered, "Hooray!"

Their first feat was done.

Jack stood and dusted himself off. He then reached up to feel what was behind the door. It was smooth. He knocked on it. It sounded like rock.

"Hand me the torch, Pierre," said Jack.

Pierre did so, and as Jack lit the ceiling above him, they could see a flat white smooth stone.

"That is my tile!" Pierre exclaimed, "We are almost inside my house!"

Jack inspected the tile looking for its edge, hoping to find a seam where he could scrape the grout away with his sharpened rock. He found none.

"The tile is larger than the doorway," Jack explained to Pierre.

"Yes. It must be, otherwise, one would fall right through. This tile is sealed to the other tile that sits on a hard floor, not an opening."

"Of course. That makes sense," Jack replied, before asking, "Do you mind if I break your tile?"

"Be my guest," Pierre answered.

In the same way that he improvised to make a chisel, Jack improvised to make a hammer. He found a larger rock this time and swung it hard at the tile above his head, until finally it was broken. At the first ray of light the men cheered. It took hard labor to find the light at the end of this tunnel. Jack worked diligently until finally, he cleared out enough space for him and Pierre to pass through.

***

Once inside Pierre's house, the men sat on Pierre's floor, at the edge of the tunnel's opening, swinging their feet in the tunnel's doorway below. After lifting themselves out of the tunnel, to that spot, they were too exhausted to move any further. So, they sat there to catch their breath.

As they sat, Jack looked around the room. The stark white marble of the floor was shinning in the sunlight that poured in from the high windows. Jack felt as if he'd just come up from hell into heaven. As his eyes focused and adjusted to the light, he began to notice what adorned the walls.

"Whoa!" he exclaimed. "Pierre, are you sure your great grandfather gave the Louvre back its paintings?"

Pierre laughed a prideful, joy filled laugh, "Every single one!"

"So what are these? These look like something I'd see in the Louvre."

"These *are* something you'd see in the Louvre, but their rightful home is here, where the painters first hung them."

"These are originals, hanging in their original places?"

"Yes! Some of the same artists who painted the masterpieces held by the best museums painted these. This house used to be a restaurant in their time. When they were alive, the artists were poor. They paid with their food with these paintings."

"And you're the guardian of this historic place, and the paintings that live here."

"Exactly! Just as my father was before me, and his father before him, and his father before him."

Jack looked back at the tunnel opening from where they had just emerged, and supplemented Pierre's statement, "Guardians to all of France's precious artwork."

Pierre beamed with pride.

Jack looked all around him, soaking up the moment and the atmosphere. "Now, I understand what you meant, when you said Sarah comes to visit a painting here."

"Yes! Sarah and David."

Jack then looked down the long hall. Several feet away, he saw a bistro table with three chairs placed in the middle of the long room, with all chairs facing one painting. It was out of place in a room that looked like a gallery (as Pierre had previously described the place), which is usually meant for strolling and observing, not sitting and eating. It was the only table in the large, long room. Jack stood and walked towards it.

"Yes, Mon amie! That is the place where we have tea, and coffee and champagne, where Sarah and David come to visit every week."

Jack's curiosity grew at Pierre's confirmation that this was their visiting place. He walked to the table and stood behind it. He gazed at the painting to learn what was so special about it. It was a sweet, romantic scene displaying a man and a woman in love, lying near a waterfall. Jack noticed the resemblance the young couple had to Sarah and David, and he smiled.

"Well, isn't that cute," Jack finally said out loud.

***

The short peaceful minutes that Jack and Pierre enjoyed, after a long, stressful journey from Sarah's yacht to Pierre's home art gallery, were quickly disrupted by Pierre's doorbell.

Pierre panicked. He told Jack to jump back into the tunnel, just in case. They threw the broken tile down the tunnel to hide it, and shut the metal door. Pierre scurried around the house trying to find a rug to cover it with. He found one. It didn't match the decor, but he didn't care. He threw it over the metal door of the tunnel, then ran towards his front door as the doorbell incessantly rang.

Half-way there, he realized he was still wearing his wet clothes that were now dirty from the tunnel, and that these clothes were the same clothes he had been seen in, while evading the police.

He stopped. "It is better to pretend not to be home," he said to himself out loud.

The doorbell nagged him again and again. He tried to force himself to ignore it. He wanted to peer out a window, but was afraid he would be seen. He tiptoed ever closer to the door, avoiding all windows. He strained his ears to listen. It sounded like the police. He ducked under an end table to make sure he could not be seen from a window.

Although he felt confident that his oversized fedora sufficiently covered his face at the airport, and although he firmly believed that his tunnel entrance, five miles away from his home, on the opposite side of an unnavigable hill, provided further impenetrable cover, Pierre feared the officers might recognize his clothing as those worn by Jack's getaway driver.

Pierre waited under the short end table for what felt like hours—his body sore from his rough travels—but it was only minutes.

Soon, the police left, and Pierre breathed a sigh of relief. He would let Jack back out of the tunnel, but he had to find a room without windows to keep him in.

CHAPTER 44

While Jack was in hiding in Europe, Gil was very busy in L.A. The stronger and bigger he could build a case against "Charlotte's" pawns, the easier it would be to get Jack off the hook with the Europeans. His main focus was to show that each of the pawns had been taking orders from a female voice with an English accent; not a male voice with an American accent.

Beth was the first to get arrested. The case against her was air tight. She now sat in a holding cell, alone, without a lawyer, still bawling from the sudden shock of learning that her boyfriend, Gil, was a police officer—the arresting police officer. He had arrested her, from the backyard of Jack's Bel Air mansion, where he had left her locked up with free reign over a fully stocked bar, after Beth had burst in with the news that spiraled into the dreadful discovery that Venus was Charlotte, and had set a trap to frame Jack for her crimes. Upon returning from Venus' vacant home to Jack's Bel Air mansion that day, Gil left Beth in the backyard long enough to complete the urgent tasks he and Sam Chapman set upon to try to regain control of the situation. When he finally opened the door to the backyard, he'd found Beth a blubbering drunken mess. Her conditioned worsened when produced his handcuffs and read her her rights.

Now, as Beth sat alone, distraught and scared to death behind the cold steel table in the holding cell, she felt the heat of Gil's glare from across the table. Gil was not the one conducting the interrogation. He left that to a different officer, Officer Henderson, who bombarded Beth with relentless questioning, as Gil sat by his side, glaring across the table at Beth. She couldn't take her eyes off Gil. He knew everything. There was no point in lying, not even if she could collet her thoughts well enough to even think of any lies—which she couldn't.

So instead, she begged. She begged for leniency. And she offered. She offered to tell a lot more than she already told Gil during their friendship.

This was good. Beth's individual criminal activity was easy to prove. She had already confessed it all to Gil in detail, essentially giving him the instruction manual for becoming inducted into Charlotte's network of pawns. Beth's prior confession was corroborated by the calls Gil received from the female voice dubbed "Charlotte" and the corresponding theft of funds from the dummy account, that had been set up for the undercover investigation, in the same manner that Beth told Gil it would occur. There was nothing more they needed to convict Beth. The purpose of this interrogation, was to get Beth to provide all her known contacts within the crime ring, so that LAPD, through Gil's leadership, could take each and every one of them down, one by one.

After leaving Beth in fear, for many hours, that leniency was not forthcoming, the interrogating officer finally gave Beth a ray of hope.

"This is a test, Beth. I'm going to hand you a pen and paper. You can fail this test, or you can pass it. I already know the answer to the question I'm going to ask," said the officer, which was a lie. "If you want leniency," he continued, "you have to pass the test."

"Well, uh, um, well, h-h-how do I pass the test?" Beth asked through sobs.

"You can pass the test by proving to us that you deserve leniency. You can pass the test by answering the question honestly and completely. If you fail to list even one name, whether you forgot it or not, so you better not forget, then you will not receive any leniency, but will receive the maximum sentence for each and every instance you stole from your employer."

Beth whaled a cry of fear as the officer continued.

"And each sentence will run after the last. The years you serve will not be served at the same time. Your first 15 years will be followed by another 15 years, then another and another..."

"Oh nooo!!!!" Beth screamed. It was the first time she heard how much time she could face.

"Oh yes, Beth," the interrogating officer said calmly, "So you better take your time and make sure you don't miss a thing."

The officer pushed a notepad and a pen towards Beth, and instructed: "You need to list the name, address and phone number of every single person you know to be one of 'Charlotte's Angels.' When you are finished with that list, you need to create a second list, and identify every single person who you *think* might be one of 'Charlotte's Angels.' Do you understand me, Beth?"

Beth nodded vigorously.

The interrogating officer continued, "And next to each name you list, you need to also list the name, phone number and address of that person's employer. Do you understand your task, Beth?"

Beth managed to squeak out a small, "yes."

"Good. Now remember, do not forget a single name."

With that final instruction, which hung in the air like an ominous warning, Officer Henderson and Gil both stood in unison and exited the room.

Once outside of the holding cell, Gil and Officer Henderson watched Beth through a one-way glass. Beth began writing profusely. She did not look up from her task for more than 45 minutes.

The two men chatted about the investigation as they watched Beth complete her task.

Gil spoke first, "The best thing about Beth's arrest, is that Beth's employer was one of a handful of high profile victims Venus used to frame Jack."

"How does that help Jack?" asked Officer Henderson.

"If we can show Beth's employer was Venus' long-term victim, we can show that Venus knew his account information and was therefore able to initiate the million-dollar wire transfer, in a scheme to frame Jack."

"So, it was Beth's employer and a bunch of Europeans Venus did this with?"

"Yes. And the dummy account we created for our undercover operation."

"Dang. She was trying to make it look like Jack stole from the investigation too!"

"Yes. Well, I think she was trying to make his alleged theft as obvious as possible, and tried to ring the alarm bells as loudly as possible, pointing the finger at Jack in a way we couldn't miss."

"So, that's why she stole millions in one foul swoop, which was a deviation from her typical skimming off the top."

"Yes. If she hadn't given us that lucky break of also stealing from Beth's employer, Jack would be in a much more severe problem right now.

"That's lucky," said Officer Henderson.

Gil continued, "Beth's confession, which provides a detailed description of Venus' activity, will give us the strongest evidence to prove Jack is innocent, and to show that he has been framed by Venus."

"Sure," agreed Officer Henderson, "And Beth can testify that neither she nor any of her co-conspirators ever knew Jack before six months ago, when your investigation began."

"Yeah. She'll definitely remember the timing of it. She'll base it off of when she initiated me, as Jack's assistant, into 'Charlotte's Angels' to begin stealing from Jack, my supposed billionaire boss from Texas, who none of them ever knew before."

"That's right," said Officer Henderson. "That is how you'll prove to the Europeans that Jack was a victim. Venus' pawns only ever knew him as a potential victim."

"Exactly," agreed Gil. "It's irrefutable evidence that all prior theft was done at Venus' hands alone."

"It sure is," agreed Officer Henderson. "The more of 'Charlotte's Angels' we can gather and connect to Venus, the better things will be for Jack!"

"We also need to establish how far back in history we can trace their criminal activity," Gil said. "This will show that Jack's appearance on the scene, only six months ago, has nothing to do with this criminal operation—other than to investigate it."

"I think we did that in the interview, didn't we?"

"Not as much as I would like," answered Gil. "With her English accent, I'm assuming Venus was stealing from Europeans before she was stealing from Americans. In addition to gathering as many pawns as we can, we have to trace their criminal activity as far back as we can, and show a pattern that I'm sure will match patterns of theft from the other big fish Venus used to frame Jack. With that connection, we'll really have a solid case for exonerating Jack."

Beth finally put down her pen. Seeing her do so, Gil said, "Let's go." Then, he and Officer Henderson re-entered the holding cell. Before they were seated, Gil grabbed the notepad from Beth. He almost hollered with joy at what he saw.

Beth had offered more information than what she was asked to provide. Her first list was even better than expected. At the top of the page it read: "Charlotte's Angels -- The ones I personally recruited over the past 10 years."

As the recruiter, Beth was an eye-witness with fist-hand knowledge of the theft committed by the people on that list! This meant they were not just under suspicion, but would be guilty as charged! There were 50 pawns listed there. In the next few pages, where Beth listed only people she merely suspected, there were 25 more names.

Gil felt like he'd hit the jackpot. As instructed, Beth had also listed the employers of all the pawns. With names and addresses of all the victims, and an eye-witness to theft from those victims' accounts, Gil could now obtain the bank records of the victims, which could then be analyzed so that patterns could be drawn. Gil would then share those patterns with the English authorities to match against patterns in their own victims' accounts.

***

All of the people Beth listed were arrested, given plea offers, and plead guilty in order to reduce their grand larceny sentences down from 15 years to 5 years in prison. Beth received the same plea offer.

In the confessions of the pawns Beth identified, each one had described a female voice with an English accent giving them orders to follow, which was later rewarded by a cash filled envelope, disguised as junk mail appearing in their mailboxes later.

Each of these confessions helped solidify Gil's case to exonerate Jack. Gil now had proof to show the English authorities that the systemic theft that occurred over the past 10 years all tied to one female voice with an English accent. He would encourage the English authorities to look for the same patterns of theft in the accounts of their victims, and to interrogate staff who held positions similar to those of the convicted thieves in L.A., who victimized their American bosses.

***

As Gil's investigation progressed, he also discovered the Golden Bartender. However, there was no concrete evidence against him. There was only Gil's strong suspicion. His suspicion was based on the Golden Bartender's presence in each bar that had misdirected refunds of purchases Gil made from the dummy account he and Jack used during their investigation. The Golden Bartender's presence occurred too often to be mere coincidence; and

Gil was leaving no stone unturned. Any hunch, any suspicion, any possibility, was a lead he would follow.

Therefore, Gil arrested the Golden Bartender, despite a lack of probable cause to do so. Bending the rules didn't matter to him, right now. If the evidence he gained in the interrogation was tossed out of court for violating the constitution, that would only hinder their ability to convict the Golden Bartender. It would not stop them from using the information to persuade the English authorities of Jack's innocence. So, Gil pressed forward as if he were trying to make the case of the century.

The Golden Bartender refused to talk without first obtaining immunity. Gil was undeterred. He invited Sam Chapman into the room to grant the immunity requested. It was a no brainer. They weren't expecting to be able to convict the Golden Bartender anyway. His only value was for more information—building a bigger, thicker file against Venus. One that showed that each and every one of 'Charlotte's Angel's' stole from their employers the same way Beth had stolen from her boss. This was significant because Beth's boss was also one of the victims Venus used to frame Jack, during her great, false heist—designed only to place a bunch of stolen money in Jack's name, while she fled, leaving Jack to be arrested for her crimes.

The Golden Bartender was granted immunity, then he sang like a canary. He knew the names and faces of 100 victims, and each of their personal assistants, who arranged through him many VIP table reservations, and who also double or triple booked each reservation. The Golden Bartender confessed to refunding the excess billings into a copycat account where he was instructed to divert the funds—instructions given by a female voice with an English accent. He confessed that he had done this for many years, and that it was always the same female voice with an English accent giving the orders. He also confessed that JAK LLC, which held the expense account of a Texas billionaire, new to L.A., who had arrived in L.A. only six months ago, was one of the many victims, from whom the female voice with an English accent had instructed him to steal.

***

Over the next several weeks, the pawns fell like dominos. Leading a team of LAPD officers, Gil lead the arrests of each and every pawn identified by the Golden Bartender. He also lead the arrests of each pawn who had attended the Aspen weekend that triggered Clifford Williams' initial call to Jack Wayne, which started the undercover operation.

The personal assistants of each of the account holders, who Clifford Williams had long suspected were victims of theft, were all arrested. In addition, Gil and a team of LAPD officers arrested several other personal assistants, personal trainers and private masseuses.

Finally, all the operatives of this extensive crime ring had been taken down. Even though the ringleader had not yet been arrested, this crime ring was taken out of commission, for good.

***

Under Sam Chapman's direction, the D.A.'s Office also took additional steps to protect the victims. The D.A.'s Office arranged for victims' advocates to counsel the victims in order to educate them about the methods these criminals used to commit theft. The victims were warned about their long-term trusted personal assistants, their masseuses, their favorite bartenders, and all the other service providers the city of L.A. offers to make people feel like royalty. This measure was taken in hopes that the education would enable the victims to better protect themselves, in the future, by asking for receipts for all bookings, and comparing them to each bank statement every month; and to use private mail boxes to which their assistants did not have access, when receiving debit and credit cards and bank statements in the mail. Sam Chapman viewed this extra precaution as a shield, lest that escaped ringleader rear up again at some point in the future, sometime, somewhere, long after the dust settles. He also hoped this shield would serve as a trap, should she attempt to reincarnate her crime ring with new and different pawns.

***

At the end of many long weeks, which Gil had spent working 20 hours a day, he sat at his desk at LAPD headquarters and hung up the phone with the last victim's advocate who reported to him that she had concluded her final meeting with the last victim on the list.

Just as he did so, the Chief of LAPD approached his desk. He congratulated Gil for a job well done in protecting the community. "Listen, Gil, your hard work, and Jack's hard work really paid off in this case. I know we didn't catch the ringleader, but I guarantee you one thing, you completely dismantled her crime ring here in L.A."

"Yeah, but..."

"No 'buts' Gil. Your mission was accomplished. If all you were able to do with the ringleader, is to run her off to a place outside my jurisdiction, well, then, that's just fine with me."

"Thanks, Chief," Gil answered, happy for the praise, but still anxious about Jack's wellbeing. The ringleader who slipped away felt like an old case now. He wasn't too upset by that loss anymore. He couldn't be. He was too preoccupied with the question of what would become of Jack Wayne.

CHAPTER 45

During the many weeks that Gil was wrapping up the investigation back home, and building the evidence to prove to the Europeans that Jack was innocent, Jack became very comfortable with Pierre's secret tunnel.

Jack and Pierre chose to play it safe until word from L.A. reached them somehow, that Jack was in the clear. Neither of them knew how long that would be. Until then, Pierre took his guardianship over Jack very seriously. He kept him comfortable and well fed, and well hidden, until it was safe to send him back home.

It was easy for Pierre to keep Jack hidden. Pierre was normally a recluse who did not allow visitors. His precious art collection was a secret from the world. That was part of his method of preserving it, and the main reason for Pierre's reclusiveness. He made Jack swear an oath of secrecy about the tunnel and the art gallery in Pierre's home. Jack did so, without hesitation.

Luckily, on the day that Jack and Pierre had emerged from the tunnel, Pierre's staff had the day off, under the belief that Pierre was out of town, not to return for several days.

Before his staff came back to work, Jack and Pierre had disguised the tunnel's entrance with a better looking area rug, covered by a long table holding it down at both ends. This covered the metal door, while still giving Jack easy access into and out of the tunnel. This was necessary because Jack went into the tunnel every time Pierre's doorbell rang.

Pierre gave his maid strict orders not to move the table or the rug, upon her return to work. She obeyed the instructions without question, as she knew that Pierre was very particular about his home and his furnishings and decor. Therefore, she didn't even find the request odd, and never knew that Jack hid inside the tunnel during her entire 8 hour shift.

Jack went through all that misery for no reason at all. Had Pierre opened the door on that very first day they emerged from the tunnel, when the police rang his doorbell, he would have learned that the police were there only to tell him that they had discovered his stolen car, abandoned by a thief, who they believed fell off a cliff and died, while evading police.

Many weeks passed before Pierre and Jack learned of this. The delay in receiving the news was caused by their caution. Careful not to alert authorities to Pierre's connection to Sarah and David, who received Jack as a fugitive from England, in flight from English authorities, Pierre waited several weeks before attempting contact with David and Sarah or responding to anyone else in the outside world.

CHAPTER 46

Gil Ramirez, Sam Chapman, and the District Attorney gathered around a conference room table with a speaker phone placed in the middle of the table, ready for a very important call.

It was a telephone conference scheduled with the English authorities who were still seeking Jack Wayne's arrest, unless and until they could be satisfied by the Americans' evidence that Jack was innocent. Their stubborn focus on Jack was mostly the result of their inability to identify the woman described in the criminal files convicting all of her pawns. Jack was the only person whose identity they knew. This made them very reluctant to let him go. He was the only one they might possibly be able to punish in their case.

If the District Attorney had been thinking like a defense lawyer, he would not have turned over so much detailed information to the English authorities to facilitate this call. As part of his strategy to prove Jack innocent, the District Attorney gave all the information about Jack's undercover operation, including the address of the Bel Air mansion, in which he had worked. The point was to show exactly when the investigation began so that the English authorities would see that Jack had no connection to any of the L.A. victims or their felonious assistants involved in Venus' crime ring until he began investigating the crime ring. The D.A.'s office had sent the complete files of every fallen pawn, which showed many years of theft from the same victims, using the same method, long before Jack's investigation began. Therefore, proving that Jack was investigating these crimes, not committing them, should have been clear cut.

However, the English authorities had performed additional investigations since they had last spoken to the District Attorney, and were now able to answer some of the questions he posed that had left them stumbling before.

For example, all fraudulent wire transfers, which were directed into Jack Wayne's bank account at the London branch, were performed from a laptop inside that same Bel Air mansion from which jack conducted his so called investigation, using the internet inside that home.

The English authorities argued this was proof that Jack stole the money. Upon hearing that accusation, Gil jumped out of his chair and shouted into the phone. "That was Venus! She placed the laptop there! I found her hair on the chair she sat in, where she planted that laptop then made those transfers! That was not Jack! That was Venus!"

The District Attorney placed a hand on Gil's arm and quietly asked him to stay calm.

When Gil sat down, still fuming, they heard an English officer say into the phone: "How do you know it was her? Did you see her?"

"I didn't have to see her!" Gil spat back.

"Then you do not know which one of them did it."

Now, Sam Chapman was irked, and he couldn't resist a smack down, "Is that considered evidence, where you come from? Not knowing who did it, is considered reasonable doubt, where I come from. Actually, it's considered no case at all."

The District Attorney, calm and poised, took over the conversation. "Calm down, gentlemen. Let's keep our heads here. We're not enemies. We're law enforcement officers cooperating on a case. What Mr. Ramirez meant, sirs, is that the reason he did not have to see her, is because he knows exactly where Jack Wayne was at the time Venus logged into that laptop and those online bank accounts to initiate those wires; and he was NOT inside the Bel Air mansion at the time."

"Can you prove that?" asked an English officer on the phone.

"We most certainly can," said the District Attorney, "and just so you know, what you have told us about the laptop and the wire transfers is not news to us. We were already aware of it. That is how we can prove to you exactly where Jack was at the time the transfers were made. He was in a country club, which in LA traffic, would put him at a location, at least one hour's drive away from the Bel Air mansion from which the transfers were made, at the time they were made."

"What evidence do you have to prove that?" demanded the English police officer.

"We have his cell phone activity showing calls made from inside that country club. We have receipts he signed when purchasing food and beverages inside that country club. And we have surveillance video footage from that country club that clearly show Jack Wayne was there for several hours during and surrounding the time that Venus made those transfers for the obvious purpose of framing him for her crimes."

"It is not that obvious to us!" insisted the English officer. "For all we know, your man became corrupted by this woman, and they were working together. You admit, and you have told us, that he was here in London with her! Sharing a hotel room! And the timing of their cozy visit is very telling. It was just after he stole the money."

Now the D.A. became angry. He raised his voice, "Jack did not steal the money! A man intending to abandon his post and run off with a thief would not give his exact location to another officer!"

Gil joined in, "That's right. I knew where Jack was at all times. I had his exact itinerary. London was the first stop before he was going to investigate a bank near the Swiss border where we have evidence Venus deposited stolen funds; and where we suspected large cash withdrawals were made in order to carry it across the Swiss border into an anonymous Swiss bank account.

We were on the brink of setting up surveillance on that bank to catch her in the act of withdrawing funds, until you interrupted our investigation."

Thick silence from the other end of the phone hung in the air.

Sam turned the knife in deeper, "Thanks to you guys, the thieves got away with all the money in that account. We tried to send a test wire to it, but the account is now closed; and the country it is in has strict laws preventing us from subpoenaing it."

More silence from the English authorities.

Sam couldn't help taunting them, "Are you still there?" knowing full well they were still there.

One man cleared his throat, "Ah, uh, yes, we are still here."

"Now," said the District Attorney in response, "Let's talk about how you're going to write up an official report making it very clear that you have exonerated Jack Wayne, and that you agree he was performing a law enforcement investigation, when the subject of his investigation framed him for her crimes."

"We can't do that before the funds are released back to their owners!"

"We can't agree to unfreeze the funds, until we get that exoneration from you," said the D.A., pointedly.

Before the call was over, an agreement was reached in which the English authorities gave the Los Angeles County District Attorney's Office everything it demanded concerning Jack Wayne.

CHAPTER 47

With Jack's passport being sent via FedEx from London to the District Attorney's Office in Los Angeles, Jack had to impose upon Sarah Cartwright for one more favor. He needed her help to get him the hell out of Europe.

Out of an abundance of caution, his colleagues in L.A. declined the invitation of the English authorities to deliver the passport to Jack's location in Europe. That was unnecessary, they had explained, and insisted that the passport could be sent to the Los Angeles District Attorney's Office. Although they had already struck a deal that completely exonerated Jack, everyone, including Jack, felt much more comfortable with the idea of getting Jack back to the U.S. without ever having to encounter European authorities. Sending the passport directly to the D.A.'s Office in L.A. kept Jack's location a secret, and also kept his friendly host clear of any suspicion.

Now, Jack needed a ride home. Sarah and David very graciously offered their private jet for transportation to L.A. Jack gladly accepted. Pierre, now a very good friend of Jack, drove him to the plane.

As Jack approached the plane, he grew more and more anxious to get home. He distracted himself with fun little details to try to make the time pass more quickly. He saw the word "Mustang" painted in large letters across the plane. This made him smile. On the drive there, Pierre had explained that

David named his plane after wild horses David adopted from Eastern Oregon. The information increased Jack's respect for David.

Seeing the name of the plane, and remembering with fondness the hospitality and crucial assistance David and Sarah gave him, Jack felt a twinge of guilt. He had once questioned Sarah's judgment of David's character. Indeed, he had even suggested that David may have been guilty of white-collar crimes involving the notorious and despicable White Jr.

It was perfectly ironic that Jack once believed Sarah had fallen in love with someone guilty of white-collar crime, only to commit that very mistake himself. Jack shuddered at the memory of his relationship with Venus.

Still judging himself harshly for the Venus mishap, he stepped onto the private plane and cursed under his breathe at the excess and luxury that greeted him inside. "One last bit of this, and I'll be back home," he mumbled under his breathe. It was not that he was ungrateful. He simply had seen enough of wealth and luxury during these past six months. It was time to get back to his neck of the woods, where he belonged—inside the D.A.'s Office, fighting crime.

***

Eager to see Jack in the flesh and safely on the ground in the U.S., Gil drove to the private airport where Jack was scheduled to land. He drove a modest Buick. This was Gil's real car. There was no longer any need to be driving a Lamborghini from the impound lot. Upon Jack's arrival, Gil graciously drove Jack home to his real house, not his fake Bel Air mansion.

As they pulled into the garage of a modest three bedroom, two bath home, Jack breathed a sigh of relief, "Ah, home, sweet home."

"Welcome back, Jack," Gil said heartily.

Jack invited Gil inside to join him for a much needed glass of whisky. Gil gladly accepted.

Once seated in the comfort of Jack's living room, a glass of whisky in each of their hands, Jack gave Gil all the details of his exciting escape from England. Then, Jack couldn't resist turning the conversation back to business. He was curious about the status of the case they had developed against Victoria, or Venus, or Charlotte, or whatever her name was.

Pouring himself another glass of whisky, Jack asked Gil, "So what were the results of your search warrant on her house in Bel Air?"

"No fingerprints. Professional 'movers' wiped it down clean. Every surface, every inch. But that doesn't matter, because in England they pulled her fingerprints from the hotel room you shared. The problem is, her fingerprints aren't in any database, anywhere. So they're kind of useless when you don't have a person in custody to match them against."

Jack asked, "She's never been arrested in her life?"

"Never. And she's never undergone a background check for any occupation or employer, either. So no fingerprints and no DNA anywhere in any database."

"Did you find anything useful in that Bel Air mansion she occupied?"

"We discovered a secret room with numerous file cabinets filled with documents."

"Excellent! Did you find lots of stolen bank statements?"

"No."

"What was in there?

"Pizza recipes."

Jack looked surprised at first, then smiled and shook his head.

Gil continued, "Yeah, it was filled with old family recipes. They were organized by country, in separate file cabinets, also containing maps and addresses of pizzarias they wanted to acquire, or locations they thought a pizzaria would do well. There was even a pizza oven in the room."

"Is this a joke?"

"Nope. The house was owned by an offshore company named Mama-mia's Pizzaria Italiana."

"Gil, Quit."

"I'm not kidding. Listen to this, the offshore company wasn't actually an Italian company at all," Gil paused and raised his eyebrows at Jack, as if to say, "get it?"

"Let me guess," said Jack, "It was in a country with more stringent financial privacy laws."

"You guessed it!"

Jack tilted his head back and sighed. He sank deeper in his soft, leather chair and took a long drink of his whisky. "So, we're never going to find her, are we?"

"No, I'd say we're not."

"Did they search the contents of the pizza oven?"

"Sure did."

"Was there any pizza dough in there?"

"Absolutely not."

"Didn't think so. What was in there?"

"Burnt documents."

"Probably all those pizza recipes that didn't work out."

Gil laughed heartily at Jack's obvious joke, along with Jack's exasperated laugh of defeat.

"Anything else interesting in the pizza oven?" Jack asked.

"Oh yes, there were melted cell phone parts in there."

"Oh, she probably just slipped and fell, and a cell phone flew out of her hand into the pizza oven."

"Yep, hundreds of them did."

Jack roared with laughter at Gil's response. It was now his turn to laugh. It was a full, hearty laugh, filled with amusement. Jack continued laughing this way for a long time, as a burst of stress released itself from his chest, through genuine laughter.

Humor was the best way to ease the pain of a lost case and an escaped criminal. Only this time, there was no following it up by saying, "we'll catch her next time."

EPILOGUE

Although Venus got away, she wasn't sure she was free.

Now seated on the bottom step of the porch of her modest home on Cyprus, she leaned against the steps behind her, and caressed the sand with her bare feet, as she watched the gentle waves of the warm Mediterranean Sea roll towards her. She rested against the upper steps on her elbows, which caused her voluptuous breasts to pop forward in a display of exquisite beauty. The red wine in the glass she held threatened to spill against her skin, which was mostly bare because of the tiny bikini she wore, which only covered the necessary parts.

She ignored the people strolling along the beach, many of whom could not look away from the seductive pose and movements of her body, which still remained an integral part of her. Though, now, her seductive nature was more of a curse, than a blessing. The desire men held for her was not nearly as thrilling as it once was, back when she used that desire to take something from them. She could no longer play that game, because it would jeopardize the sanctuary she created for her retirement from a life of international crime.

As Venus watched the waves roll towards her, one, after the other, after the other, the unceasing repetitive motion made her eyes glaze over, as her mind wandered towards strange and uncomfortable thoughts. She thought of

Napoleon Bonaparte. Her chest tightened at the frightening thought that, like him, her final days would be spent incarcerated on a small island.

She tried to quell the rising panic attack with another sip of wine. It worked.

But her mind wandered back to Napoleon. Did his British guards poison him? Or did he die of a broken heart? If he died of a broken heart, would Venus also die of a broken heart? Napoleon's last words were, "France, the army, head of the army, Josephine." These were the dying words of a man who longed for lost glory and power and love. Venus had lost all that, too. "Josephine" was the last word Napoleon uttered. The name of his wife. This, Venus thought, was proof that Napoleon died of a broken heart.

Unlike Napoleon, Venus' incarceration was self-imposed. Long ago, she had selected this charming little home, on this slice of paradise, to serve as her retreat if the day ever came that she had to evade authorities in Europe and the U.S. It sounded like a good idea at the time. The quaintness of the home would not draw attention, and certainly did not look like it hid millions of dollars of stolen money in the hidden bunker beneath a trap door, under the pantry in the kitchen.

The charming little home was a good idea—as long as she was free to come and go as she pleased. But now, the threat of being recognized, or hunted in the Western Hemisphere forced Venus to limit her movements to this island in the Eastern Mediterranean, that she had never travelled to through commercial carriers, and where she had always used an identity never used anywhere else on earth. The island was so far east that the next land mass she could see across the water, was Syria.

What once felt like a heavenly paradise, now felt like a forced exile to a far off, remote and isolated place that she could never leave. Staring at the waves rolling towards her, Venus wondered if this really was better than prison.

Even worse than the feeling of incarceration, was the torment that Jack Wayne left in her mind.

Out of the corner of her eye, she saw him! Suddenly, she jerked up spilling the wine onto her long legs, as she quickly turned her head to look directly at Jack. Exhilarating emotions burst inside her. Confused emotions. Strong emotions mixed with the eagerness to run towards the man she longed for and loved, conflicted with the instinct to flee from an authority figure who might really capture her and incarcerate her. It happened in a split second. It was followed by the crushing disappointment that always came, whenever she saw him. As her eyes focused, in the second that followed, she could now see. It was not Jack. It was never Jack. It only ever looked like him from the corner of her eye. Sometimes it was a man with dark hair like his. Sometimes it was a man of his height, and build, or a man who had a similar gait. Sometimes it was nothing at all. Just her imagination. But it was never Jack.

Shaking off the trauma of yet another false alarm, Venus looked at her now nearly empty wine glass. There was enough left for one more sip. Something to clam her nerves, after the hundredth false alarm this week, alone. As she brought the glass to her face, the smell of the wine triggered nausea. "Oh, no. Not my wine too," Venus lamented. Even wine was starting to lose its appeal. She now worried that the loss of yet another one of life's pleasures was becoming permanent. Today was the first time this happened so late in the afternoon. It was an annoying new development that began during these first few months, after she abruptly and dramatically parted ways with Jack.

Usually, this sickness, triggered by smells she previously enjoyed, only happened in the morning.

END

PROSECUTORS-LA SERIES

Prosecutors-LA is a series, which mixes the genres of Romance and legal Thrillers. Each book can be enjoyed independently and out of order.

The series follows the lives of fictional L.A. prosecutors whose personal lives sometimes collide with their cases. Naturally, drama ensues—then, strict enforces of the law suddenly find themselves in scenarios they never would have imagined—sometimes playing the part of defense lawyer, resorting to street justice, or becoming a suspect on the run. The glitz and glam of Los Angeles, and its residents' favorite international destinations add further indulgence.

Stay up to date on new releases in the series, by joining fan club at: Summer.Augustine.club

In Chronological Order:

Book 1: *A Brush with Love, A Brush with the Law*

Book 2: *White Jr.'s Trial*

Book 3: *The Suspect*

Book 4: *The French Art Heist*

OTHER BOOKS BY THIS AUTHOR

A Brush with Love, A Brush with the Law

David is a hard-partying Hollywood millionaire who has maintained a long-standing reputation as a sexy, charming and lovable womanizer. Though he thoroughly enjoys his bachelor lifestyle, David's secret desire is to become a family man—a dream constantly sidetracked by the allure of Hollywood. Then, David begins to experience close encounters with Sarah, a highly accomplished, conservative and well-respected Deputy District attorney—who is a virgin. But the close encounter that rattles David's world the most is the close encounter he has with the criminal justice system, which threatens to take his liberty for a very, very long time.

White Jr.'s Trial

Sarah Cartwright and Kelly Luthan have one goal in common: Get White Jr., convicted of rape and attempted murder. Their motives are as different as their lives. Whether these women are justified, is a question only the jury can answer. Readers of this book will be the jury.

You will judge White Jr.,—a handsome, wealthy, young man who was raised by a good family with the highest level of integrity. You will assess the credibility of his accuser, Kelly Luthan—who is now rekindling an old flame, after many years of being apart, and is deathly afraid that the trial will reveal to her beloved fiancé, the fact that she was once convicted of prostitution. You will debate the mystery of Sarah Cartwright—the prosecuting attorney who ordered the arrest of White Jr., then immediately disappeared.

When these two women first set this case in motion, they never imagined that the unyielding call of the criminal justice system would draw them from their happy lives and threaten everything they hold dear.

The French Art Heist

Their favorite painting is gone! David Nolan stands accused. Who else could have done it? It was Renoir's painting of the future—David's future with Sarah, predicted and painted in 1890. According to David, it depicts the future and the past. Having seen it for the first time in 2015, he swore it captured the most precious moment in David's love story with Sarah when they first met. Livid and out of his mind with rage, the painting's owner demands: "No one else had stronger motive to steal it than David!" there's just one problem—he himself is David's alibi. So, who really done it?

ABOUT THE AUTHOR

Summer Augustine is a trial lawyer of 20 years, who began her legal career in criminal law, as a prosecuting attorney. She later became a civil litigator, handling complex business law cases. She is no stranger to the courtroom or the background drama that brings people there. She hopes to share her passion for the law, life and love with her readers through a series of novels, *Prosecutors – LA*, which is also being developed for a television series. (The novels can be enjoyed independently and out of order). Sumer Augustine has lived on the west coast of the United States her whole life. She loves world travel, art, and history. She spends her free time sipping champagne by the pool, unless her nieces and nephews are visiting, then it's tea parties and remote control airplanes.

To follow the author on her various social media accounts, please visit her website: SummerAugustine.com

Stay up to date on new releases, special offers, book clubs and other events, by joining her fan club: SummerAugustine.Club

www.ingramcontent.com/pod-product-compliance
Lightning Source LLC
Chambersburg PA
CBHW030358310726
48979CB00001B/360

* 9 7 8 0 9 9 6 8 6 8 6 7 9 *